CW01637904

HAUNTED HIDEOUT

MICHELLE DOREY

THE HAUNTED ONES BOOK 1

Copyright © 2018 Michelle Dorey

All rights reserved.

ISBN: 978-1-988913-07-0
Monarch Moments
Cover Design by Juan Padron
https://www.instagram.com/padrondesign/
Edited by Paula Grundy
https://paulaproofreader.wixsite.com/home

DEDICATION

As always, to Jim. If it weren't for you I'd still be living the cubicle life!

CONTENTS

ONE

"I have to take this. Sorry." Lydia shrugged, lifting the cell phone to her ear as she walked out of the house.

Everything about the century home, even such detail as the scent of baking bread in the oven, was staged. So was the phone call. The young couple would be anxious to make an offer if they thought more buyers were interested in the place. She didn't win the Florida Realtors Award every year for nothing.

Her hand threaded through golden locks as she looked down at her high-heeled foot tapping on the walkway. From the Armani-tailored, raw-silk suit to the Jimmy Choo shoes, it was all about the image—juggling clients, closing deals and immense success. Give the middle-aged doctor and his trophy wife a few more minutes alone in the house, and they'd be begging her to write up an offer.

Her eyes flashed wide at the squeal of tires from the black Suburban suddenly appearing at the end of the walkway. She could only stare as two dark-suited men raced up the walkway. It was right out of a movie!

The older guy paused and peered down the street while the younger one gripped her by one arm and flipped an ID case with his free hand. "FBI. Come with us."

She yanked away from him. "What? There must be some—

”

“You’re Lydia Robbins, right?” The older guy’s voice was low and gravelly. His dark-brown eyes peered at her like she was his next meal; squinting in borderline pleasure.

Her heart thudded against her rib cage. Was it that deal last week, the hotel she’d sold? Some kind of money-laundering scam? She held her chin high daring them to charge her with something. She was innocent in all that, by God! “Yes, I’m Lydia Robbins.”

The younger guy flipped his badge closed and pulled her toward the idling Suburban. “You’re in danger, Mrs. Robbins. Hurry. Get in the vehicle.”

Her heel twisted when he tugged her, and she scrambled to stay erect. “No! I’ve got clients inside. I have to—”

The older man moved in. “You have to come with us. Now! If you don’t, that’s the last house you’ll ever set foot in. They’re coming and it’s not to buy a house.”

Her gaze ricocheted between them like watching a ping pong match. “Who’s coming? Who are *they*?” But her feet clattered fast keeping up with them. The back door of the tank-like vehicle was thrown open wide. Strong hands clasped her elbow, ushering her inside.

A black guy behind the steering wheel turned his head. “Move! Move! Move!”

The door had hardly banged shut before there was another screech of tires, and they hurtled forward. She gripped the handle above the door, hanging on for dear life as the car spun around the corner. Her mouth was suddenly dry and she croaked, “What’s this all about? Are you sure it’s me you want?”

The older guy in the front seat dropped his head and sighed. He turned around and in a gentler voice replied, “I’m sorry to break this to you but your husband...he’s dead. We found his body in a canal off Cypress Avenue.”

His words kicked her in the stomach. She slumped over, hardly able to breathe. No. It couldn’t be. There had to be some kind of horrible mistake. “No. My husband is in

Bermuda on business. I don't know who you found, but it wasn't Liam!"

This time it was the younger agent beside her who spoke, "Mrs. Robbins. We've been working with your husband for some time. He didn't want to involve you. But I'm afraid his cover was blown. Castinadas got to him before we could. I'm sorry."

Every cell in her body filled with rage. She spat the words, "I don't know any Castinadas! Liam works for a hedge fund! He's an accountant, for God's sake!" She flipped her phone up and hit the button to call him. This was a joke! A mean and cruel joke.

A tinny message told her that the message box was full. She blinked a couple times looking at it. That didn't make sense. Liam was fastidious about his phone, always clearing out old messages. There was some mix-up or something. She hit the button about to try again, when the young agent's hand covered hers.

"I'm sorry, but it was your husband's body. Liam was working for a drug cartel. We contacted him and made a deal. He was going to testify in exchange for immunity. You and your family were to go into the Witness Protection Program

The world stopped. She sat like a stone, his words echoing in her brain. Liam? He was dead? He'd been working for some drug lord? But he was an accountant not some Mafioso guy! She'd teased him this morning when they spoke on the phone. With the sale today, she'd actually be making more money than he had all year. She'd kidded him she was going to get a pool boy.

Oh my God. Liam. Gone? Tears welled in her eyes.

The young agent passed her a tissue. "Other agents are picking up your son and daughter. The Castinadas are ruthless. They don't stop at just the snitch. They go after the whole family."

Her mouth fell open, the breath frozen in her chest. Oh my God. The kids! Her heart lurched to her stomach.

TWO

She raced forward when the elevator doors slid open. Ahead of her were paper-strewn desks, men and women perched behind them, peering at computer screens or talking on phones. Her heartbeat sounded in her ears blocking out the cacophony of the busy office as her eyes searched the room.

"Where are my damn kids!" she bellowed. The office went quiet, and a woman at a desk pointed a finger.

There! They were in a glass-walled office behind the main entrance. She lurched forward, her knees suddenly weak. Thank God, they were safe!

"Mrs. Robbins?"

She ignored the man who had stepped forward and rushed past him. Through the glass of the far office, she could see Mark rise to his feet. He raced for the door, her daughter right behind him.

As she strode to get to them, her mind was flying ahead. Had they found out about their father's death the same way she had—from some FBI agent? Oh shit! Did they know?

Both kids came to a skidding halt in front of her, clutching her arms with white-knuckled fingers.

"Mom! What's happening?" Angela's whispered words spoke volumes. Even though she was fifteen, in that moment she was a child looking for the safety that only a parent could give. And Lydia was now the only parent.

"Can we go home, Mom?" Mark's fingers dug into her arm, tugging fiercely while tears flooded his eyes.

Lydia took a deep breath and hugged her children closer, holding on for a scrap of sanity and time. How could she tell them their world had just ended along with their father? Especially Angela. She'd always been Daddy's little girl.

The agent she'd dismissed so easily was back, holding the office door wide for her. He nodded, giving her the room and space to be alone with her children.

Lydia nudged her kids, guiding them to the private sanctuary. "It's okay. We're going to be all right." But she was saying it more for herself than them. Nothing was going to be okay ever again.

When the door snicked closed behind her she closed her eyes for a moment, fighting the tears. She sniffed and shook her head a little to clear it, looking into their frightened eyes. "I'm so sorry... Oh God. Your father is gone."

Angela pulled back and her face screwed tight, "What do you mean gone? He's in Bermuda, Mom."

Lydia shook her head and sobs wracked through her. She had to gasp out the news. "No. He isn't. He's...he died." Better than saying he was murdered. But just barely. Murdered! Oh my God.

"No! That can't be. There's some mistake. *He's not dead.*" Angela words rushed out, her head shaking back and forth.

Lydia looked down at Mark. His eyes spanned wide and his face had gone pale under the sprinkling of freckles. He took a step back from them and clamped his lips shut. She reached for the eleven-year-old and pulled him in; burying her face in his dark curls as he stood perfectly still. Mark...his iron self-control was in full display. This would kill him and he would never let on.

Angela wailed, clutching at her mother. "No Mom! Daddy? Pleeeease! It can't be true! Noooo!"

They stayed like that for a long time, just holding on to each other. Mark's tears were silent while Angela railed at the world and herself for not being nicer to her father. She could have, should have spent more time with him; told him she loved him more often.

Remorse turned to anger. Angela pulled away, swiping the tears away with the back of her hand. "So why are we here? Was Daddy in trouble? Did they do something that caused his death?" Her eyes narrowed glaring at the people working outside in the main area.

Lydia slumped into a chair, pulling Mark onto her lap. She never wanted to let go. He needed her and she needed him. She looked up at her daughter and sighed. This was going to be hard. "Your father was working with the FBI. He was trying to do the right thing. The men where he was employed...they were bad. They were a drug cartel. When your father found out, he was going to testify against them." How long had he known though?

Angela's head tilted and she leaned closer, "Harmony Group is a drug cartel? *A drug cartel?*" She pulled up a chair and sat close to her mother and brother. Her eyes were narrow when she continued, "They killed Daddy, didn't they? They found out he was going to tell and they killed him."

Lydia took a deep breath. "Yes. And now they're after us."

Angela's jaw dropped, while Mark pulled away gaping at his mother. Lydia sat straighter, and her hands rubbed their shoulders. "We're going to be okay. Your father made sure of that. The FBI are going to protect us just the way they would have if your father had lived. Your dad helped them, and now they're going to help us."

But Angela wasn't buying it. She crossed her arms in front of her, her head pivoting around their surroundings. "How? They couldn't save Daddy! How are they going to help us? Drug cartels are ruthless, Mom. They could kill *you* while you're showing houses...or Mark, when he's riding his bike to school. I'll come out of a friend's house and some sniper will put a bullet in my brain."

"No! They won't know where we are. We'll be in the Witness Protection Program. A new state and new IDs." Lydia tried to sound positive even though it took every last iota of energy.

Angela jumped to her feet. "Where? *Alaska*?"

Lydia could only stare at her daughter for a few moments. Angela had come pretty close to hitting the truth. "Not Alaska. Up north in New York State. Some town near the border."

"What border? Massachusetts or Connecticut?" Mark ventured a whispered question.

Again, it was hard to keep the sadness from her voice. "Neither. The Canadian border. Some place called Alexandria Bay."

Angela shook her head, tears once more in her eyes. "Great. When do we leave?"

But before Lydia could answer, the FBI agent who'd been assigned to them opened the door and popped his head through the crack. "We need to hit the road in twenty minutes. The sooner you're out of Miami the better."

None of them had the energy to respond. Like chain-gang convicts, they quietly trudged out of the room behind the agent.

Each step drawing them closer to an even worse nightmare.

THREE

Lydia's hand rested on her son's shoulder as they were guided into another room, this one without windows. And a uniformed agent stood at the door—holding a machine gun.

"Everyone take a seat," the guard said, holding the door open, then closing it when they entered. Lydia heard the tiny snick of the door latch locking. She closed her eyes and pressed her lips together. This was for real, *real*. The three of them flopped into metal chairs bolted to the floor around a stainless-steel table—also bolted to the floor.

The door to the room opened, and this time it was a woman who stepped in. Her dark eyes were kind, set in a face that although attractive, showed signs of wear. "I'm Special Agent, Rhonda Bowles." She looked at Mark and Angela and her head fell to the side. "I'm really sorry about your dad."

Angela fingered a fresh set of tears from under her eyes. She nodded and put her hand on her mother's shoulder. Mark didn't even try to respond, his mute focus on the floor.

Lydia pushed up from the chair, setting her son on his feet

in front of her. "So this is it? We're leaving now? Can we stop at the house to pick up some things?" But it wasn't the designer wardrobe she was thinking about. There were photo albums, memories of the kids as babies, toddlers and then there were the family photos with Liam. Liam sitting next to the pool, shading his eyes from the sun and trying to turn from the camera's lens.

The room seemed to spin when she pictured that. There'd be no more easy teasing, no more holding each other sharing their day. Her grasp on Mark's shoulders tightened for a few beats as she fought for control. Looking down at her son's dark curls, was another reminder of Liam, the same mop of unruly hair.

But Liam was gone. From now on it would be her providing emotional support for the kids. She took a deep breath and looked over at the agent. The small shake of the woman's head told Lydia that their past lives were over. There'd be no photo albums or memorabilia to anchor them. They were adrift.

Angela stepped closer to the agent and her voice was flat. "I can't call my friends to say goodbye, can I?"

"I'm sorry, honey. I'll need your cell phones." She looked past Angela, meeting Lydia's red-rimmed eyes. "We can't take any chances with your safety."

Lydia scooped her phone from her pocket and handed it over. It was tempting to take one last scroll through the pictures she'd saved there, but it would bring on a new onslaught of crying. There'd be plenty of time for tears later.

In the elevator taking them to the basement parking lot, Angela slipped her hand around her mother's. Lydia looked down at her and managed a smile meant to be encouraging. Her son kept his distance, being stoic, watching the numbers light up on the elevator's overhead panel. Her hand curled over his shoulder pulling him closer. Her children were all she had now.

***

The female agent, Rhonda, rode shotgun while her partner, Alex, drove the same black Suburban Lydia had been in before. Thankfully both agents were sensitive enough to stay silent as the vehicle threaded through the streets.

It was a somber ride, all three of the Robbins family sitting mute. Lydia stared out the tinted glass at places, her mind flooding with memories the familiar scenes evoked. All their lives, Miami had been home. It flew by in a blur of tears. Everything reminded her of Liam. Restaurants where they'd dined, parks and the white sand beach where they'd enjoyed weekends with the kids. All gone now along with him. She turned and leaned forward, her hand on the seat back next to Rhonda.

"What about Liam's funeral? There has to be *something*." Her voice cracked, choking on her next words, "*We can't just leave him as if he never existed*!"

"Oh God, Mom." Angela buried her face in her hands, rocking back and forth, moaning softly.

Rhonda turned and her voice was low. "His body will be cremated. I'll arrange for his ashes to be sent to you. I'm afraid that's the best I can do."

"What about Aunt Carla? Won't she wonder what happened to Dad? To us?" Mark's voice was barely audible. He looked down at his lap, shredding the tissue in his hands.

Lydia sank lower still. Oh God. With all that had happened she'd never given a thought to Liam's sister and her family. She and Carla had never been close but still, the kids would miss her. What would Carla think when she couldn't contact any of them?

It was the other agent, Alex, who answered, glancing into the rearview mirror. "We've done this many times before. Don't worry about your aunt. I'm sorry, but you can't ever contact her. She's in Denmark, right? We didn't deem her to be at risk."

Thinking of Carla brought to mind the other people she'd never see again. There was no other family but there were friends she'd worked with. Although she'd miss them it would be nothing to what her children would suffer. Angela had a big social network but it would be Sophia she'd really miss. They'd been inseparable since kindergarten. And Mark. There were only two friends he'd hung around with, but they were tight as bark to a tree.

Now there was no one. They only had each other to console and cry with over Liam...Dad.

How long had he known about the drug cartel? Had he known when he was first recruited by Harmony Group? And to have kept this from her, for the last nine years? He had a secret life that didn't include them. But for sure they were now paying the price. Lydia closed her eyes and her lower lip trembled.

Liam. How could you do this to us?

FOUR

Angela

Angela was numb, the barren trees and yellowed grass skimming by as she stared out the window, barely registered. They must have been in the car close to fifteen hours. She was cramped and sore. There were no tears left to cry, only an empty hole inside that would never be filled again.

Mark broke the silence. "Are we stopping soon? I need to go to the bathroom." To prove his point he squirmed in the leather seat, causing her to edge closer to the window away from him.

The woman agent's assurance that they'd stop at the next service center was just background noise. When her mother reached across and touched her arm, Angela turned to face her. For just a fleeting moment the grief and loss in her mother's eyes caused an ache in her chest. How would Mom ever manage without Dad? He'd been the rock that they all depended on to keep the household running. Mom was always busy with her career, working crazy hours. Dad was the only one to pry Mark away from *Minecraft* so he could get some fresh air and exercise. Her brother would probably retreat even further into the cyber world, if that was even possible.

"Angela, you should eat something." Seeing the blank look on her face, Mom turned to the woman agent. "Rhonda, do you think we could stop and get some warmer clothes? I mean it's November and it's going to be cold right? Can we go to some kind of mall?"

Yeah clothes. Angela looked up at the female agent waiting for an answer. The jeans she had on felt old and repulsive. Not to mention the light cotton sweater that was full of tears, snot and sweat. Eew. She'd never be able to wear these things again...not without thinking of Dad. And then getting dragged into the FBI office and learning about his death. This whole thing was a nightmare.

Rhonda turned and smiled at Mark, "If you can hold it for another twenty minutes, there's an outlet mall we were going to stop at." Turning to Mom, "We're meeting up with another agent who will take you from there. He's got your new identity papers and credit cards, along with new cell phones. You can eat something then shop for some things. The house will have everything you need but you're right about the clothes."

Angela leaned forward when a new thought bubbled to the surface. "Wait. We don't get to pick our names? What if I get some kind of weird name like Stella or Tiffany? No way am I going to be a Tiffany."

"I want to be Logan. That's a cool name." Mark actually grinned.

Angela shoved him into their mother. "That's not cool. It's dumb." Trust Mark to come up with something stupid like a movie character.

Alex chuckled and his eyes showed in the mirror. "Sorry dude, but the names have to be bland and boring. We don't want you to stand out in any way."

Angela sniffed at her brother and turned back to the window. Great. She was probably destined to be Mary. Or worse—Ann. Please God, not Elizabeth. Her stomach rumbled, bringing her back to the here and now. A picture of a hamburger flashed in her mind. She hadn't eaten since lunch the day before! And getting out of the stuffy vehicle to stretch her legs would be nice.

Her eyes closed and her gut sank down to her knees. Dad. He was gone and there she was thinking of her belly and stupid names. She'd give anything to have him there with them.

***

Mark silently continued to pick at the hangnail on his thumb. He didn't give a shit about what name he was going to get. Dad was dead, and Angela was worried about her new *name*? What a jerk. He closed his eyes falling back into himself as he always did when things got to be too much. A small sigh tried to get out his mouth but he shut it down.

Dad was the only one who ever "got" him. It was okay to be quiet, unlike his sister, always yammering going on about her friends or some lame movie. Who would understand him now? Mom still treated him like he was in preschool. Hell, he was finishing middle school, the top of his class in math and science. Angela would probably go on to college...if there was a scholarship for *shopping*. As if.

Dad had always balanced out the "squees" and chatter of his mother and sister. Now he was gone. He'd left big shoes to fill. How much had he known about the drug world? Were the FBI right, that they'd be safe? That never happened on *Narcos*. The innocent family always got killed. Maybe he should get a gun. Mom wouldn't have to know. He could order it online.

He popped his head up and reached over the seat before him. "How big is this town we're going to be living in?" Mark nudged Alex's shoulder. Although, would the town size matter if the drug cartel was still searching for them?

"It's a lot smaller than Miami, my friend. Maybe forty thousand people or so. It's a touristy kind of place." Alex smiled and then his gaze drifted back to the road.

"Like Disney World?" His chin dropped lower. Nice place to visit but he wouldn't want to live there. Too much flash and people making like the fantasy was real. Shallow and boring.

This time it was Rhonda who spoke. She was nice like Arnie's mother had been. God. He'd never see Arnie again. Or his mother.

"It's a busy place in the summer with boaters. It's on the St. Lawrence, right on the border. But there's a friendly town atmosphere that you'll like." She turned and smiled at him. "There was a time when drinking liquor was illegal in the States. But not in Canada. People used to smuggle booze in from there and sell it over here. They were called rum runners. Alex Bay was one pit stop for them. That's kind of exciting, right?"

His mom shot Rhonda a look, "Maybe not, considering why we're going there." She took a tissue from her purse and blotted it on the bloody nail, he'd picked at.

Rhonda's face became still and she nodded, turning back to face the front. "Yeah. Sorry. I just thought it would make the place sound more exciting than it really is."

Mark shrank deeper into his seat, sensing the tension that had fallen like a shroud. It all came back to Dad. How was he ever going to get through this?

FIVE

Jake

Jake Whitaker nursed his second coffee, sitting at the table in the food court. In the sheepskin jacket and jeans, he could be any guy waiting for his wife or girlfriend to take a break from shopping to join him. Except for his eyes. It was a habit he'd formed from his years with the Bureau. He could tell you how many elderly couples and young mothers with squalling babies were seated there, even down to their eye color, height, age and clothing.

He fished his cell phone from his jacket and glanced at the time. When Rhonda had called they were twenty minutes away from the outlet mall. They were late. Could be traffic, or maybe not. He'd read the file and he knew the reputation of that drug cartel. But Rhonda and Alex were seasoned agents. If anyone could get the family out of Miami without being trailed, it would be them.

When the far end of the glass doors popped open, a sense of relief eased his tension, watching Rhonda stride through. Behind her was a slender blond in a summer business suit, herding a dark-haired teenage girl on one side and a skinny boy about twelve or so on the other. And of course, securing the rear was Alex.

He raised his hand and got to his feet, signaling to them. Rhonda smiled and then said something to the blond before leading the way over to his table. With just a glance their tear streaked and weary faces tugged at his heart. They were not only dealing with grief, but shock from being ripped from everything familiar and secure.

Rhonda smiled and leaned in to give him a quick hug. "Hey Jake. How you doin'?"

He held her at arm's length and looked into her bloodshot eyes. "Better than you from the looks of it."

She snorted, "At least I'm goin' back to warm weather, my friend." She turned her head and motioned the blond closer. "Lydia, I'd like you to meet Jake Whitaker. Don't let appearances fool you. He may look easygoing and a bit rough around the edges, but he's got eyes in the back of his head. You'll be in good hands."

Jake took her small hand in his. "Pleased to meet you. I'm sorry for your loss, Mrs. Robbins." Without waiting for Rhonda to continue, he turned to the daughter and reached for her hand. "Angela. I'm sorry about your dad."

When she nodded, he turned to the boy. In a microsecond he knew this was the one who was hurting the most. This was the one he'd have to watch carefully to keep him from slipping into depression. Years of dealing with families and kids gave him a Spidey sense about these things. "Mark. This is tough, man. I'm sorry." He held on to the kid's hand a beat longer.

He leaned to the side and extended a chair for Lydia, "Please, have a seat."

She smiled, revealing thousands of dollars invested in a perfect set of teeth. "I'm afraid, Mr. Whitaker, my son needs to use the restroom. Long drive." Her hand cupped Mark's shoulder and she started to turn away.

Angela grimaced and stepped over to her mother. "I'm going too. I feel grungy. I need to wash my hands at least."

The other agent clapped him on the arm. "You stay here, I'll stand watch at the restrooms, man." Alex was pretty cool for a guy who'd been awake for more than twenty-four hours, but what the hell. Jake sat back in his seat.

He watched the small troupe cross the food court and then disappear down a corridor marked with a sign for the washrooms. He sat down and finished the rest of his lukewarm coffee. There was a reason that the mall was the meeting spot; it was busy with people coming and going, but more importantly, totally anonymous. But an afternoon of shopping with two women and a young kid wasn't something he looked forward to. What guy ever did?

***

Mark sat next to the new agent, waiting at the front of a department store for his mom and sister. The last he'd seen them they were pushing a shopping cart almost filled to the brim with clothes. But considering what they'd gone through in the last while, at least it took their mind off the bad stuff. For a little while, anyway.

"Hey Mark. What do you do for fun? Are you into sports?"

He jerked in his seat at the agent's friendly intrusion. "Uhhh..."

The guy shrugged and his mouth pulled to the side in a lopsided grin.

Mark glanced at his feet and then at the man, "I like video games?"

The guy...Jake, yeah, Jake was his name, grinned wider still and turned slightly to face him. "Oh yeah? Like *Skylanders* or *Pokemon*? I've tried *Skylanders* a few times and it was fun."

Skylanders? That was for amateurs. Mark shook his head, "No...uh, *Minecraft*. You build stuff, like even the pyramids or the Eiffel Tower. But monsters or zombies can attack anytime. It's cool."

"Really? Sounds fun." Jake got to his feet and stretched, throwing a smile down at Mark. "C'mon. This store must have tablets or an Xbox. Might just as well throw it in the cart while we're at it."

Mark's mouth fell open and he jumped to his feet. "Really?" He thought he'd left any chance of getting a new tablet for the game behind. Mom wasn't crazy about the time he spent playing even though his grades didn't suffer. Dad had been the one to convince her to get it. His stomach fell, thinking of his dad.

"Sure. Your mom's going to need a laptop anyway, and I'm sure your sister is normally glued to her phone, so we'll take care of the electronics." He nudged Mark's shoulder with his elbow. "They're busy clothes shopping. They wouldn't even think about computers. We got this."

Mark nodded and followed Jake through the aisles until they got to the electronics department. The area flashed a bit with the TV monitors and computers running, but Mark spotted a shelf of laptops. Great! There was an Aspire Switch like the one Arnie had. He tugged it forward, his fingers running over the keyboard.

Jake sidled closer "Hey, I thought you were going to get a tablet." His blue eyes were narrow looking down at him, but there was that same quirky grin.

"This is actually better. It comes apart..." Mark unhooked the screen and held it up to the agent. "See? A tablet but you can use the keyboard for the game. No plugging in keyboards and stuff. My friend Arnie got this for his birthday."

For a moment the guy's smile faltered and Mark's gut fell a little thinking he'd say no. But, instead Jake nodded. "Sounds like the right way to go then. " He bent to reach behind for a boxed unit and handed it to Mark. "Now for your sister and your mom. You pick out what they had before. Deal?"

"Sure." He kept his voice level, even though he was already picturing how he'd recreate the castle and improve on his game.

***

Lydia wheeled the shopping cart up to the line of registers. She jumped when Angela nudged her with another cart. Her eyes flitted past the cashiers to the area where she'd left Mark and that agent. Her heart leapt to her throat not seeing them. Oh God. The drug guys? Were they here?

"Hey Mom!"

She spun around and her hand flew to her chest seeing Mark race up to her, the agent wheeling a cart behind him. "Mark. Where were—"

"We got computers for us. Well, for you and me. Angela's is a phone."

Lydia's hand rested on her son's shoulder. The kid actually cracked a smile and his eyes were clearer, excited even. If that silly *Minecraft* game could help get him through this ordeal then who was she to judge?

She looked past him at the agent who bobbed his eyebrows high and nodded. Yeah. Good call on his part. He must have kids of his own. Did he and his family live in that town, Alexandria Bay? She hoped so.

Wheeling the cart to the checkout counter, she began unloading clothes for the cashier to scan. Lydia was about to reach in her pocketbook to grab her wallet when the agent appeared next to her.

"I've got this." The smile had dropped from his face and he shook his head.

She sighed. Of course. She couldn't use the credit card because Lydia Robbins didn't exist anymore. She took a deep breath to get a grip on herself before a fresh onslaught of tears gushed. No. Not here. She took Mark's arm and went to the end of the checkout, waiting for everything to be bagged.

She'd change later. That was one thing she agreed with Angela on. She could burn the Armani suit for all she'd ever wear it again. She'd never forget the day, and she'd never wear that outfit again.

SIX

Jake

Jake wheeled the Toyota Highlander onto the express heading north on I-81. He glanced over at Lydia, now decked out in a down parka, even wearing red wooly mittens. The poor woman had no idea what was in store for her in the North Country after living in Florida all her life. He glanced in the rearview mirror to see the kids faces glued to their new devices. He might as well go through the drill while they were driving.

He reached down beside his knee and then handed the thick folder across to her. "You'll find new IDs for each of you in here. Your last name is Robertson. Close to Robbins, so easy to remember. We're changing your name to your middle one. From now on, you're Elizabeth, or short form, Liza. Close but different. The kids will keep their first names. It's too easy for kids to draw a blank when their new name is called, like in class or something."

Angela snorted, "Great. Sorry for your luck, Mom. Or should I say, Liza?"

He glanced in the mirror. Good. They were following the conversation. "There're credit cards, a driver's license and birth certificates. We've opened an account at the bank for you with a balance of ten thousand dollars."

Lydia's eyes were wide when she looked over at him, "But what about my accounts in Miami? There was a substantial deposit, investments, the kids college fund. And..." She took a breath, "...the life insurance."

He glanced at her, noticing the set of her jaw, trying to keep her composure. "The bureau looks after all that. Your savings and investment accounts are closed. The money from that, along with the proceeds from the insurance policy, will be credited to your account." He paused for a moment. The next part was always tricky.

"But you need my signature to withdraw any amount larger than two thousand dollars." She was about to protest, staring wild eyed at him, so he quickly added, "We do this for your protection. You need to keep a low profile. And believe it or not, before we made that rule, we had people try it alone. They took their money and fled, trying to make a new life on their own. It never worked out for them."

Her eyes narrowed, "How long does that restriction last? Not forever, I hope. My kids will be going to college and I really don't want you to cosign on that! No offense but..."

"It's just for a few years. At least until we know you're safe and settled." He glanced over at her. She didn't look happy about it but at least she was keeping quiet. "We've got a job lined up for you at the Department of Social Security. It's clerical and the hourly rate is fifteen dollars."

"What? You've got to be crazy! Do you realize I earned close to a hundred grand last year? Fifteen dollars an hour! Right." Her face had darkened which even the fading light outside couldn't conceal.

"Wait! You didn't let me finish. We top you up. But you have to understand that living in Miami costs more than here." He glanced out the window at the rolling vacant land beside the highway. "A lot more. Taking that into consideration you only need half of your income to maintain that same standard of living." He glanced over at her. Yeah, she was hurting but not financially. Pretty spunky. She'd do okay.

"We'll see about that." She turned and gazed out the side window, running her fingers through her hair.

"What about the school? How many kids go there? Is it some Podunk kind of place?" Angela had leaned forward, her hand on the seat next to his shoulder.

He blew out a long breath through pursed lips, "Almost three hundred." He braced himself.

"Are you shitting me? My school had three thousand kids! Oh maaan."

He decided to let it go. "Your house is on the outskirts. It's four bedrooms and right on the river. There's a few acres of land and an outbuilding, a barn. Great place to have a dog or a cat. What do you say, Mark?" The boy had been too quiet. The odds were pretty good that the kid never had a pet, and if he did it was probably a bird or a gerbil. Pets could be therapeutic.

"I'm allergic to cat dander." Mark's voice was barely above a mumble.

"How old is the house? Does it have a modern kitchen? A garbage disposal, dishwasher?" Lydia peered at him closely.

"It's turn of the century. An artist couple renovated it from top to bottom with every convenience you'd need or want. They did all that work and then moved to California. Weird." He didn't bother to add that the place had sat vacant for almost a year. The ever budget-conscious bureau had picked it up for a song on the off chance they'd need it.

With the money they saved they could afford to give him a raise. And here was this woman complaining about her income, more than he made and he risked his life to do the job.

"Maybe they were in the witness protection program." Lydia flashed a grim smile at him.

SEVEN

Angela

Angela sighed. They were on the outskirts of the town, if you could call a smattering of stores and a few low office buildings, *a town*. There were practically no lights of houses or businesses breaking the walls of pitch-black on either side of the road. It had been a few miles since there'd been any signs of civilization. Where the hell were they going to be living?

The vehicle slowed and turned down another equally darkened road but instead of the smooth pavement, this road was pitted and bumpy.

Jake's voice sounded as worn out as the road they were on. "We're just about there."

"This really is isolated." Mom's voice was also road weary, but with an undercurrent of worry. She gazed out the side window and let out a long sigh.

Angela leaned forward, peering out the front windshield. Slices of the white house showed between the trunks of thick, ancient trees, lined up in a row like sentinels. When they parked next to the walkway, a set of steps led up to a veranda and the front door, where a lone light above cast dim light. Above, two windows like eyes stared down at them as if they were intruders or something.

Jake opened his door and paused, glancing over at Mom. "You stay here while I check things out and get the lights on." When he got out and stepped forward, a handgun was in his fist.

Mark nudged Angela's shoulder, watching with eyes the size of golf balls. The fact that Jake had his gun out was a stark reminder of the circumstances which had brought them to the old house.

"I hope he doesn't just dump us here and then leave," Angela muttered. The thought of going in there stranded without a clue where they even *were*, made her shudder.

Mom sighed. "I'm sure he won't. This is his job, right?" But her mother didn't sound all that convincing.

When Jake opened the door and disappeared inside, Mom leaned over to click all of the car locks. It wasn't just her then, feeling like a sitting duck surrounded on three sides in the inky-black night. Their mom felt it too. This total darkness was definitely foreign. There were always the glare of lights in Miami. How did people in the country stand it?

One after another, a series of lights flared in the downstairs windows, marking Jake's progress through the house. It wasn't long after the upstairs was blazing with lights, that he strode through the door and then bounded out to the car. Angela flipped the lock and got out. Her leg muscles stretched, relief spreading after the long drive. The air was chilly but not frigid like she'd feared.

"All clear, just as I figured, but why take chances, right?" Jake slid by her to get the packages of clothes from the back.

She looked up at the upper level and then continued up the steps, following her mother. The house was old, nothing like the modern ranch bungalow she'd grown up in. Even the smell inside was weird, and the wooden floorboard creaked when she walked across it peering up the wide set of stairs. Her mother's feet clattered, going down the hallway while Mark was right on her heels.

"Angela, come and see this." There was a trace of excitement in Mom's voice.

Angela shrugged seeing the agent come into the entryway, his arms laden with their purchases and then joined her mother and Mark. She stepped into a huge kitchen with a granite counter, modern cabinets and an island eating area to the side next to a wide set of windows. Her mother was busy trying the faucets and inspecting the dishwasher, while Mark stared into the refrigerator taking stock.

"This is better than I'd expected." Her mother continued scanning through the cabinets and opening drawers.

Jake came in, and his hands were on his hips looking around. "There's not that much food. Just staples to get you by for a day or so. We'll go in town tomorrow to get your car and then you can get whatever you want." He wandered over to the window and pulled the curtain back. "You can see the river from here, y'know."

Angela looked over but of course there was nothing but black showing in the window. "So are you staying with us tonight?" This was uppermost on her mind right then, forget the view and the modern kitchen.

"Absolutely. I'll be a fixture for a couple of days to make sure you're okay here." He walked over to stand next to Mark who was now rummaging in the fridge's drawers. "There's pizza in the freezer and lots of soda."

Mom managed a wan smile, "And wine too, I hope." She stepped over to Angela and put her arm over her shoulders pulling her in close. "Let's finish the tour and then I'll put pizza in the oven."

There was an arched doorway at the side of the kitchen that led to the dining room. It was furnished with a long dark table, six chairs tucked in and a side cabinet. Two large windows at the side looked newer than the original set in the kitchen.

"I'm not sure how much entertaining we'll be doing." Mom sniffed and then steered them out to the front hallway. "A center-hall plan. Typical for this age of a house." She was going into real estate mode. Oh no.

Angela pulled away from her and stepped into the living room. There was a fireplace at the end of the room while a new beige set of furniture, a sofa, love seat, and chairs clustered around a squat wooden coffee table. A reddish oriental rug broke the monotony of the dark wooden floor. She shivered and pulled the collar of her jacket higher. The room definitely needed that fireplace going. It was a lot chillier in there than it had been in the rest of the downstairs.

Again, there was an archway leading to a small room, lined with bookshelves but completely bare of furniture. She went back to the living room where everyone else was.

"We left that room unfurnished. You might want to use it as an office or library or whatever. You'll be here for a while and in case you want to put your own finishing touches on the place, we just left it."

Mom looked over at him. "That kitchen update must have cost thousands of dollars. And all the floors have been refinished and new windows? That's not cheap. Funny for that couple to spend all that money and then just up and leave. They must have been loaded."

Jake's eyebrows rose and he looked away for a few beats. "I'm afraid they focused mostly on the downstairs. The upstairs is almost all original, except for the master bedroom."

"Do we have Wi-Fi?" Mark was looking after his priorities, after checking out the contents of the fridge.

"We'll get you connected in a day or so. This was kind of short notice, buddy." Jake sighed and looked down at his feet.

Yeah. Short notice for Dad as well. Angela took a deep breath and then trudged out of the room, filing past everyone and making for the stairway. Dad was dead and here they were discussing the internet and renovations in the house. *It was sick.* The whole place and everything sucked. She clomped up the staircase, the squeaks of the boards grating her last nerve.

At the head of the stairs she looked into the bathroom and caught a glimpse of a white pedestal sink and a toilet. Stepping inside there was a huge bathtub with claw feet and a curved shower rod above it. Oh God. It was probably the only bathroom, and she'd have to share it with the rest of them.

Turning away, about to leave, she jerked back at the image in the mirror over the sink. There'd been a face there! A girl with long dark hair!

She peered closer, but now only her own face, framed by disheveled brown hair showed. What the hell? Her heart skipped a beat, and she blinked a couple of times before checking the mirror once more. Nothing now. God. She was so tired and worn out that she was seeing things.

She left the room but her chest was tight, her heart still pounding fast. The first room she came to after the bathroom had to be the master bedroom. It was huge, kind of like they'd taken two bedrooms and made one large room. A queen-sized bed dominated the space, while a wall of mirrored doors concealed what had to be the closet area. Again the windows at the side of the house, the side where Jake had said the river was, were expansive.

At the sound of her mother and Mark following up the stairs, she turned to continue exploring. She'd definitely stake a claim on the next biggest room before her brother had a chance. A quick glance in the following bedroom confirmed her suspicions that the master bedroom had gobbled up the space. It was little bigger than a walk-in closet!

Her fingers trailed over the railing above the stairwell and she entered the room at the front of the house. It wasn't as big as her room back home had been, but it was probably the best she was going to get.

There was a double bed with a cream-colored spread and a large chest of drawers. She glanced out the window, looking down at the front driveway and the back half of the vehicle. The spindly tips of one of the trees outside whispered over the glass. Her eyes narrowed. She'd have to do something about that. If the wind picked up it would be sure to tap and she'd never be able to sleep.

As she walked across the worn planks of the floor, the

creaking of the wood shadowed her. Something else she'd have to take care of with a rug or something. But the closet was bigger than she would have expected. Even though the door was narrow, it went back on one side a few feet. Enough room for her stuff.

At the sound of footsteps near the doorway she turned. Mark stood in the entrance, his dark eyes roaming over the room from the window to the far end.

"No way. This room is mine, Mark. You don't need as much space as I do." She walked over to him and crossed her arms over her chest, defying him to object.

He shrugged dismissively. "Mine's closer to the bathroom anyway." With that he turned, ceding victory.

She ambled over to the bed, plopping down to test it. The new wood in the frame squeaked just a little in protest, but other than that, it would do.

Her mother stepped in, gazing around before turning to her. "This is okay, right? We'll get some carpeting and..." Her voice trailed off and she sighed. "Look, I know this is hard. I hate this too. But what choice do we have?"

Angela rose and walked over. The wear of the day showed in her mother's eyes and the deep lines creasing her forehead. She took her mother's hand and squeezed it. "It's okay, Mom. You're right. We don't really have a choice."

She looked past her mother when Jake's footsteps sounded coming down the hallway. Everything kind of echoed when anyone moved. That was annoying.

He held out the shopping bags. "I don't know which is which here, ladies. You sort it out and I'll get the pizza going."

Which brought up another question, since he was making himself at home there. "Where are you going to sleep?"

He set the bags down and then his hands slipped into the back pockets of his jeans. "Downstairs. I'll take the sofa. It's only for a night or two. It won't kill me."

Her mother's head tilted to the side. "Do you live in Alexandria Bay? Do you have family nearby, Jake?"

The smile fell from his face and he turned to leave. "Nope.

Not anymore."

Angela looked at her mother, waiting for his footsteps to pound on the stairs and he was out of earshot. "Well that was awkward. Not anymore as in dead or—"

"Not everyone is like us, kiddo. He's probably divorced. We'll just leave that alone, shall we?" Her mother reached for the first bag and peeked inside. "This one's yours."

EIGHT

Mark

Mark finished putting his new clothes in the dresser and then slumped looking around his new room. The white walls and the lacy curtains were so yucky. Even the bedspread was wussie, a baby blue with white stripes. He wandered over to the small desk and flipped the laptop open. A long sigh escaped. Until they got the internet, it was totally useless.

The sounds of drawers banging shut as Angela and his mom sorted through the new clothes, putting them away, pulled his gaze from the computer. It was kind of like the time they'd rented the beach house on Sanibel Island, getting settled in for a week of fun. Except there were no white sand beaches here. And Dad wasn't here either.

This was anything but fun. He tightened his eyes, squeezing them shut as tight as he could. He wasn't gonna cry; if he started, he'd never stop.

It was unreal to be unpacking, to actually now live in the middle of nowhere. Not unreal. More like a nightmare that you couldn't wake up from.

He left the room and went downstairs. The smell of baking pizza got stronger with each step, till his mouth watered. In the hallway leading to the kitchen he discovered a door he hadn't noticed the first time. A sliver of light shone under it. He paused, about to turn the handle to see if it was another bathroom, when the door creaked open by itself, drifting toward him. His eyes popped wider and his breath hitched in his chest.

His hand slowly rose to pull it wider. It wasn't a room though. There was a small area before another old set of stairs which led down to the cellar. That's what they call it, right? A dank and musty smell wafted up and cobwebs clinging to the wooden studs fluttered as if from a breeze. The light from the bulb did little to reveal anything beyond the first few steps. Everything below was shrouded in darkness.

"Mark."

He just about jumped out of his skin when the agent spoke. "That's just the cellar with the furnace and water tank. I was going to show it to you guys tomorrow. You'll want to know where the electrical panel is in case you blow a breaker."

When Mark turned to look up at him, puzzlement showed in Jake's eyes. Mark stammered for a moment trying to shake the creepy feeling that had skittered up his spine. Why had the door opened on its own like that? He swallowed hard. "A cellar?" He'd been right about the name.

Jake nodded and then his eyes cleared. "Yeah. Of course. You probably didn't have them in Florida, right? They're common up here to store stuff and it's where the utilities usually are kept. It's not the nicest spot in the house, that's for sure." He signaled for Mark to step out and then he flipped the switch before shutting the door. "C'mon, and get yourself a soda or something."

Mark didn't have to be asked twice. He'd check it out tomorrow when it was daytime. A cellar, huh? He could probably creep Angela out with that.

Mom and Angela's footsteps sounded on the stairwell as he

followed Jake into the kitchen. He grabbed a pop from the fridge and sat at the table.

Jake took the pizza from the oven and nodded to Mom and Angela. "That was good timing. Have a seat."

***

Twenty minutes later, Lydia poured her second glass of wine and pushed the empty plate to the side. Dinner had been a quiet affair, with Jake the only one talking, giving them more information about the town. He'd probably have to repeat himself the next day as the three of them were lost in their own heads, coming to terms with all of this. Sitting at a strange table, in a strange house with a strange man cooking dinner, was mind-bending enough. Take into account the circumstances that brought them all together and it was pretty much surreal.

Jake cleared the table of dishes and then turned to face them, "I'm going to get my sleeping bag and retire to the living room. I've got some calls to make and then I'll catch up on some reading. I'll lock up and see you guys in the morning."

"Thanks Jake." What more could she say? Whatever resources she could muster had better be spent helping her kids through this. When the agent disappeared through the doorway, she placed her hand over Mark's. He was the one who would bury the hurt rather than getting it out there to heal. "How are you doing, buddy?"

"I'm okay, I guess." He stared down at the table, while his body slumped lower in the chair. He looked up at his mother for a moment. "When do we have to start at this new school?"

"There's no rush for that; don't worry about it. You'll go when you're ready and not a minute before. Trust me on that." Lydia forced a reassuring smile and patted his hand. The kid got good grades so if it took a week or two, so what? It was bad enough to be dealing with his father's death let alone be overwhelmed with new kids at a new school.

Angela picked at the tab on her can of soda. "Did *you* know that Dad was working for that drug outfit?" Her daughter's blue eyes were still puffy from all the tears she'd shed.

"No! I'd bet even your father didn't know when he took the job. Believe me, the worst thing your father ever did was maybe speed a little. He never even cheated on his taxes and he had the smarts to do that." She took a sip of the wine. Maybe that was the problem. Liam was clever when it came to accounting but he'd never had too many street smarts. If he had more, maybe he wouldn't have been killed. If he'd been up front with her, she could have helped him.

Angela was quiet for a few moments, fighting the tears before she blurted, "I hope he gave the FBI enough to nail those bastards." She knotted her fingers together. "Cos if he did, then he wouldn't have died for nothing."

Mark glanced at his sister and then mumbled, "Will we really be safe here? What if they find us?"

She leaned forward, squeezing his hand and taking her daughter's fingers as well. "Your Dad didn't die for nothing. He gave the FBI enough evidence that they put us here! He trusted them to see that his family was safe and we have to believe that. That drug cartel will have their hands full dodging the authorities to even give us a thought. And that's thanks to your father." From the hollow feeling in her gut she wasn't sure if she was trying to convince them, or herself.

Mark rose to his feet. "I'm tired, Mom. I'm going to bed now."

She pulled him in and kissed his cheek. "Okay baby. Sleep as long as you want. There's no rush to get up in the morning. Sleep is the best thing for you right now." His fingers slipped from hers when he turned and walked slowly away, his head down. He was going to have a hard night.

Angela stood up as well. "I'm going to shower and then go to bed too. I feel like a steam roller went over me and then backed up to hit me again. This sucks." At her mother's raised eyebrows she sighed, "I know you hate that word but it's true." She leaned over and hugged Lydia before slouching across the room and going through the doorway. She was going to have a hard night too. Hell, they all were.

Lydia finished the rest of her wine and then got up to rinse the glass. Yeah. Angela was right. This totally sucked. She turned off the lights and went up the stairs to her own room and the empty bed which she'd have to get used to.

NINE

Jake

The next day Jake tossed the sleeping bag aside and sat up, running his fingers through his hair. Sleeping on the sofa wasn't the most comfortable night he'd ever spent but considering his career choice, he'd been through worse. Long, freeze-the-nuts-off-in-a-jeep kind of nights on stakeouts came to mind. He needed to use the bathroom in the worst way but there was no way he wanted them up any earlier than necessary. They'd been through the wringer in the last seventy-two hours. As a kid he'd done some camping out, and standing behind a tree wasn't all that bad.

He got to his feet and grabbed his jacket before wandering down the hall to the back door. When he stepped outside, it was cold, but the sun's rays caught in the frost blanketing the backyard. There was a huge lilac bush at the corner of the house that he could sneak behind to the take care of the ache in his bladder.

An old dirt track where a tractor or wagon used led to a barn about sixty feet away. His head pulled back seeing the wide plank door in the center of the weathered building, swaying open. He could have sworn that it was closed the other day when he brought the groceries out to the house. He zipped up and then walked down the path to check it out. Without even having to think about it, he slipped his hand to his back and drew his gun.

He stepped inside cautiously, his gaze darting from a low workbench at the far end to the stanchions once used for cattle and horses. The smell of hay and manure even years since there'd been livestock still wafted faintly. Dust motes flittered in the rays of light from a few windows high above the loft. A mouse disturbed by his footsteps darted across the floor to its hole in the corner. Other than the mouse there was no sign of life in the still and quiet space.

He turned around and flipped the old latch into slot at the side of the door. Considering the shape it was in, a gust of wind could have easily caused the door to open.

When he was about to leave, he paused for a moment watching a freighter lumber through the sparkling river, on its way through to Lake Ontario and probably Detroit. Whenever he saw them, that old song, *Wreck of the Edmund Fitzgerald* always popped into his head. Great. Now it would be an ear worm that he'd have to endure all day.

Worse still were the reminders of Claire that always stirred to the surface when he heard the sad song. The folk singer at the bar had been playing it the night he met the girl who would become his wife a year later. People had given them weird looks when it was the tune of the first dance at their wedding. But that was ancient history. Their marriage had sunk the same way the old Edmund Fitz had sank.

He shook off the memories and walked back to the house. When he entered the kitchen he was surprised to see Mark already up, sitting at the table eating cereal. He rinsed his hands under the faucet and commented, "Aren't you the early bird. How are you doing today, buddy?"

"Okay," he mumbled, chewing the crunchy breakfast. In the plaid pajamas, his tangled head of curls hung over the bowl like a he was a cocker spaniel.

Jake filled the coffeepot with water and then set about scooping the grounds into the machine. "I'll follow up on the internet and cable today and see if they can maybe speed things up." When that didn't get a response he tried another tack. "There's a rocky beach at the edge of the property. Ever play at skipping stones on the water's surface, Mark? I could show—"

"My dad and I did that when we rented a cabin at Four Creeks." The boy sank lower over the table.

Well that hadn't gone well. Jake slipped his hands in the back pockets of his jeans. "I was out to check the barn earlier. It's kind of neat." He poured a mug of coffee not waiting for it to finish dripping through. "Would you like some juice or a glass of milk?"

"No thanks, I'm good." Mark sat back and stared at him. "Think you could teach me to shoot?"

Jake's head jerked back. Where had that come from? "Uh...I don't think that's a good idea. First of all your mother would hate it and I'd have to agree with her. Guns aren't something to play around with."

"When did you first shoot one?" Now the boy was all ears, leaning forward.

"Not until I was twenty-one. Why the interest in guns? Your dad wasn't, was he?" But he already had a pretty good idea about Liam from what he'd read. The guy was an accountant in the big city. Not someone you'd connect with a gun lover.

The cloud once more descended over the kid's attention. He shrugged and then got up to rinse his bowl. "I don't know. I just thought being out here in the country, I should know how to shoot a gun." He looked over at Jake, "Dad wasn't into guns. But maybe he should have. Maybe he'd be alive if he'd been carrying a gun."

So that was what this was about. Jake sat back, setting the mug on the table. "Did you know more people are killed in gun accidents at home than ever in any shoot-out with bad guys? I know where you're going with this, but Mark, you're safe here. It's a quiet town and the drug guys won't find you."

He sat forward again and locked eyes with the kid. "Think about it, Mark. In all of this big country, finding you and your family is like finding a needle in a haystack. There's no trace of Mark Robbins anymore. And do you have any idea how many Robertsons there are in this massive continent?"

Mark nodded his head and then set the bowl in the dishwasher. "Got it. Maybe I'll get dressed and check out that barn and the yard."

But Jake wasn't entirely certain that the boy was really giving up that easy. The boy probably considered himself the man of the family now; doing what he thought would protect his mother and sister. He was too young for that kind of responsibility. Being a kid these days was tough enough without jumping into a man's shoes. This thing with guns and growing up too fast was something to watch, that was for sure.

TEN

Mark

The agent was on his cell phone when mark walked by the kitchen. After a quick shower and donning the new clothes, Mark was already sick of the house. Getting outside, breathing fresh air would be an improvement. He closed his eyes and shook his head before going out the back door. As much as he hated this place, it was home now. But when he was old enough he'd go back to Florida.

At first he'd thought Jake was kind of cool but now he knew the truth. He was just like all the other adults, treating him like a baby. Just because he was small for his age and skinny, didn't mean he couldn't be tough—or smart. He could probably beat that FBI guy in an IQ test if he had to. He was smart like his father had been. He was going to be tough and not let anyone play him for a fool. Not like those drug guys had done to Dad.

He kicked a stone on the path to the barn sending it flying twenty feet to prove his point. Ignoring the sharp pain in his toe, he looked around at the expanse of the backyard. On one side the boundary was marked by a split-rail fence and on the other the dark blue of the river. A cold breeze nipped at his face and he pulled the collar of his jacket higher.

He flipped the latch and tugged the barn door open. The only light in the dim building flowed from a few high windows and the door where he now stood. But it was enough to show a ladder perched against a half-story, open platform, above. They called that a loft, he thought to himself. There was a thick gray rope dangling from a pulley of some sort. He gripped the line in his hands and yanked on it, lifting his feet from the floor and swinging back and forth.

Skidding his feet on the floor he scuffed up a cloud of dust. When his nose began to itch, he stopped swinging and rubbed it. The ladder was next. He wandered over to it and began the twenty-foot climb to the old hayloft. He'd seen pictures of barns of course but this was the first time he was ever in one.

BANG!

He almost fell off the ladder when the door slammed shut. His heart leapt to his throat and he darted back down. Racing over to the door, he pushed on it, saying a silent prayer that the latch hadn't caught. What had caused the door to shut? He was trapped and no one would ever hear him yelling. At first it wouldn't move. He lurched and tugged at it with all his might, yanking at the stuck door. Without warning it flew open, and he stumbled forward almost falling flat on his face.

He straightened and then looked at the door feeling a chill race through his body. It wasn't that windy outside that it would have slammed the door, was it? He looked up above the door and only then noticed the horseshoe hanging above it. Unlike what he'd always seen in books, this one was upside down. Or maybe that was the way they did things up north.

The back of his neck prickled. All of a sudden the barn held little appeal.

He brushed his hands together and then looked out to the water. The frozen grass crunched under his feet as he walked across the yard, heading for the shoreline. Squinting at the sun sparkling on the water, he peered across to what looked to be an island, dark evergreens topping a rocky shoreline. To the left was another island, and he squinted harder seeing the peaks of a structure that looked like a castle. Yeah, it was definitely a stone castle on that island. The north's attempt at Disney World's Cinderella Castle? He's have to ask Jake about that.

The beach was carpeted with smooth stones making it hard to walk. He had to look down picking his way across until he was only a few feet from the water, gurgling in small waves against the rocks. He spotted a flat rock about as big around as a golf ball. Picking it up, his fingers curled around it and he let fly, smiling when it skimmed the surface, kissing the water four times before disappearing. He tried another and another, before spotting the perfect stone.

He stepped a few feet to grab it and then stopped short seeing an old man walking halfway up the long stretch of beach. Where had he come from? He hadn't noticed him before. And there was no sound of him walking along the rocks.

A flat, gray hat slung low over the guy's forehead, and his shoulders were hunched in a bulky, dark coat, his hands in his pockets. He just stood there staring across the water. Mark gazed past the old man trying to see if there was a house or car to indicate where he'd come from. But all he could see was the low-lying shoreline, bordered by fields with the odd tree. His house was the only one around.

He hurled the stone across the water. Should he go back to the house to get Jake? Even though the guy was old, and just watching the river, he had no business on their property. What was he up to? He made like he was getting another stone but his gaze slid up the shore to take better stock of him to give Jake a better description.

He dropped the stone and then jerked upright. The guy was gone! Mark peered down the beach and then across to the fields, but there was no sign of him at all. What the hell? He was too old to get away that fast.

Mark walked quickly across the beach and then broke into a run when his feet hit the grass. He had no idea where that guy had gone and he wasn't taking chances. Not with the reasons they were here in the first place...no way, José. He had to get Jake. Now.

He raced up the steps at the back entry and yanked the door open. When he stepped inside he was panting, trying to catch his breath. Mom was just coming down the hallway, still in her robe and pajamas.

She took one look at him and her mouth fell open. "Mark! What's wrong?" She held him by the shoulders, while her eyes inspected his face. "What's the matter?" Her eyes sparked with fear and she looked out the door behind him.

He deliberated all of two seconds whether to tell and upset her before blurting, "There was some old guy just up the beach from me. One minute he was there and then the next second he was gone."

Jake stepped out of the kitchen and stood next to his mother. "Where?" He grabbed his coat from the hook and then slipped it on. "Never mind. I'll check it out. You guys stay here." He pushed past them, one hand reaching for the door, the other sliding to the small of his back. There was a gun in his hand when he stepped outside.

ELEVEN

Lydia

Lydia's hands shook when she pulled Mark into her body. Her poor baby had been outside all alone and...and some guy was out there? With one arm still sheltering his, she reached for the door latch and flipped the dead bolt. Herding him into the kitchen, she raced to the window, just in time to see Jake stepping out from the grass onto the beach. His hand was outstretched holding his weapon.

When Mark sidled close, joining her in watching the beach area, she turned to him and her words rushed out in a torrent, "Did he come near you? What was he doing? Did he say anything?" Her heart thudded fast in her chest while she fought hard to keep her voice even and steady.

"What's going on?" Angela was at the counter. She hadn't even heard her enter with her feet in thick socks. "What're you looking at?" She stood on Lydia's other side, pulling the curtain wider.

"Mark saw someone at the beach just now. Jake is gone to check it." She stepped back and then raced across the kitchen and down the hall. The front door was probably locked but she had to make sure! Her fingers twisted the knob but of course it was locked. She looked into the living room on her way by peering at the window, and Jake's sleeping bag still spread on the sofa. He was going to be staying a few more nights until he could say with absolute certainty they were safe!

She sprinted back to the kitchen; the kids were still hunched at the window. "Anything?" She clutched their shoulders when she stepped between them, her face close to the clouded glass. She swiped it clear.

"No." Angela turned to her brother, "What were you doing out there all by yourself? That was a dumb move."

"He's coming back." Lydia saw Jake shake his head, seeing them staring out the window. But instead of coming in, he strode out of sight at the back of the house.

"He's probably checking the barn." Mark shrugged the coat from his shoulder and set it on the back of the chair. The blue of his eyes were rimmed in white; he was still so shook up. He walked into the dining room and stopped at the window, cupping his hands to the glass and watching the area outside.

"Maybe Angela's right. Until we know what's what around here, no wandering off outside by yourself. Understood?" Oh my God. What would she have done if Mark had been hurt? Until Jake came back in the house, they weren't out of the woods yet.

"K." His voice was muffled but at least he was agreeing. The poor kid was scared to death.

At the pounding on the front door, her hand flew to her throat. Mark raced to the door. "Make sure it's Jake before you open it!" she yelled.

But still she hightailed it right behind her son.

"It's me!" She recognized the agent's voice and opened the door.

When he stepped inside he cupped his hands in front of his face and blew some warmth into purple-tinged fingers. Even the top of his ears were red from the cold air outside. "You sure you saw someone, Mark? There wasn't a sign of anyone that I could see; no footprints anywhere or any tire tracks either. You said it was an old man? What was he wearing?"

Mark met his gaze without faltering. "I saw a guy. *Honest.* He had on this cloth-type hat that was like a tam or something, and his coat was dark. It hung almost to his knees. He kept watching the river like he didn't even know I was there. I turned away for a second and then he was gone!"

Jake looked over at him for a moment, the doubt clear in his puzzled eyes. "I believe you saw something Mark. But maybe it was a bush or tree that kind of looked like a guy? We're at least a half a mile from your closest neighbor. And if someone was there, I would have seen him walking away. The barn was clear and no sign of any vehicle other than mine. I checked it too."

Mark's face had regained its color and then some. His cheeks were tinged with angry spots of red when he turned and raced up the stairs. She was about to follow him when Jake's hand on her arm made her stop. "Let him go. He needs some space. I'll talk to him later. Maybe we'll go outside and check the beach from where he stood. It might have been a trick of the light or...I don't know, a bush?"

She took a deep breath trying to tease the knot of worry in her chest loose. Mark wouldn't make this up. He was truthful almost to a fault sometimes. But he'd been through a lot in the last seventy-two hours. Maybe he thought he saw something, but that description had been pretty detailed for it being just a bush.

"I'm getting something to eat." Angela spun on her heels and went back to the kitchen.

Lydia scowled after her daughter. "I need a coffee. I'll talk to Mark later. If you go to the beach with him, Jake, I'm going too." She shot a cold glance at the agent. How hard had he really looked? Was he any good at his job? But, the other two agents had sang his praise, that he was one of their best. So far, she wasn't impressed, dismissing her son's claims that easily.

"I'm going to make some calls. Let me know when you want to go into town." He slipped his coat off and hung it on the hook by the door. He fished a set of keys from his coat pocket and walked silently into the living room, shoving them into his pants.

All this and she hadn't had a cup of coffee yet. She blew out a long sigh as she walked down the hall to join her daughter.

TWELVE

Lydia

When Lydia entered the kitchen, Angela was rummaging in the cabinet.

The girl flicked a packet of hot chocolate powder, and a wan smile flashed. "Seems like a good morning for hot chocolate. We need to turn the heat up in this place." She mixed her drink and then popped it into the microwave before looking over. "You don't think there was really anyone out there do you?"

Lydia sighed and poured a coffee. "I don't know what to think. I trust Mark. But that agent didn't see anyone or a sign of anyone. I'm going to check it myself when I get dressed."

At the beep of the microwave, Angela pulled out the mug. "Y'know… it *could* have been a bush or something. Have you ever noticed Mark squint sometimes? Maybe he needs glasses." She popped bread into the toaster and then leaned against the counter, sipping the hot drink.

Lydia stirred her coffee but her hand paused at Angela's words. She'd never noticed that about Mark, yet her daughter...a girl who had always been caught up in a busy social life, had. What kind of a mother doesn't notice her kid squinting trying to see things in the distance? How had she never noticed? "That's news to me, Angela. He never mentioned that it was hard to see the blackboard at school or—"

"He *wouldn't.* Bad enough he's scrawny without wearing glasses *too.* How much of a nerd would he look like then? Besides..." Angela's voice trailed off, "...you were always working. You never would have noticed."

Oh God. It was the truth. The only surprising thing was that Liam hadn't noticed either. Surely if it had been that bad he would have. But then again, Liam was busy trying to stay alive and keep them safe. Shit. Here she had thought the FBI agent was incompetent but it might just be Mark's eyesight. If anyone was incompetent it was *her*, as a mother.

She sat down at the table next to Angela. "I'm sorry. I did work a lot and maybe I wasn't there for you guys as much as I should have been." She took a deep breath. But that would change. Hell it *had* to change, considering everything that happened.

Angela surprised her when she placed her hand on hers. "It cost a lot to live in Miami. You did what you had to do. And maybe Mark's eyes aren't that bad. Dad never noticed, did he?"

Her eyebrows bobbed high and she nodded. The kid had a point. Actually two points. The extra income she earned had meant the difference in living in a better neighborhood and taking a two-week vacation every summer. Lots of their friends hadn't been able to do that. "Well, I won't be working insane hours anymore." She snorted and smiled at her daughter. "Imagine *me* working in an office, nine-to-five. I'll get used to it though, I suppose." It would be mind-numbing, pushing paper rather than working with the public, but at least she'd be around more for the kids. She sure wouldn't miss the Church-of-the-Open-House, every Sunday trying to move dud houses.

"I hope we can get the internet hooked up soon. It's going to be so boring out here without it." Angela finished the last gulp of her chocolate and then looked down at the table. "I wonder what Sophia thinks. Or actually any of my friends. I just vanished into thin air without warning."

It was a whole lifestyle and circle of friends to grieve about. If Angela, who was strong and resourceful was hurting; what must Mark be going through, missing Arnie and David? In an ironic way, it was a blessing that all of the children's grandparents were long dead.

Instead of having a second cup of coffee, she got up. "I'm going to get changed, and see how your brother's doing. Then we're heading to town for some more stuff. You want to come along? The sooner we get ready, the sooner we can leave. Maybe we'll get Jake to drive us by the high school so you can see it."

When Angela nodded and walked over to the sink to rinse out her dishes, she added the coup de grâce. "I'd like your input on the car to buy. In another year you'll be driving it, you know."

The wide smile on her daughter's face was a welcome change.

***

Jake glanced up when the two women walked by the living room to head upstairs. He got up and walked to the entryway, placing Lydia's new set of house keys near her purse on the hall table. He tossed his own keys at the other end and then peeked out the window in the door. Still, there was only the Toyota parked out front, no sign of any movement or tracks in the frost.

The mother was having second thoughts as to his ability to protect them, but that was okay. Far better that she supported her son right then. The kid had seen something, but it sure hadn't been some guy gawking at the water. There wasn't a soul around. It had to be a trick of the light or maybe his imagination.

He glanced at the stairs, hearing the murmur of their voices before the small bangs of drawers shutting signaled they were getting dressed. They had a full day ahead, getting more groceries, the banking and cruising car lots. With any luck, they'd be ready soon to get on with it.

This relocation assignment was a pain in the ass. He was an FBI agent for Pete's sake! And here he was, out in the middle of nowhere, playing nursemaid to the family of a dead guy. He shook his head. What a drag; ferrying them around, acting like a tour guide, holding their hands as they eased into a new life...what a tedious pain.

He wandered down the hall to get a coffee. As he sipped it, he stood at the kitchen window looking out at the rocky shoreline. There were a few outcroppings of trees and low-lying scrub cedar that the kid could have mistaken for a man.

But the kid had also described a cap and even such detail as the guy's hands in his pockets. That didn't sound like he'd seen some bush or something. Unless the kid was acting out a bit, looking for attention. That wouldn't be unheard of with these kinds of families, especially for the kids involved.

Still. He gulped the coffee and then strode from the room. One more check outside wouldn't hurt. As he passed the door to the basement, he noticed that it was ajar and the light was on. He could have sworn that he'd shut that door and turned the light off last night. He darted his eyes to the left and right. The guy outside, now this?

He slipped his gun out and stepped inside, peering into the dim space at the bottom of the stairs before he flipped another light switch next to his head. Immediately, the gray cement pad at the bottom showed along with the electrical panel and a washing machine and dryer. He inched down the stairs, his gaze arcing over the musty room while a ticking sound just barely audible, pulsed. At the last step he noticed the laundry tub, and the steady drip of water falling from the tap.

He jerked to the side when a cobweb floated against his cheek, his hand scraping at the threads. Yuck. If there was one thing he hated, it was bugs. Little by little he made his way across the room, leaning to the side to check beside the furnace. Darkness was the sole occupant, aside from a centipede or two. There was nothing down there. He was about to put his gun away when a creak on the ancient steps made him spin, aiming it.

It was the boy! Mark's eyes flared wide and his feet pounded on the stairs, racing up.

"Hey! Wait." Jake's shoulders slumped as he tucked the gun back in his holster. Shit. Mark finding him in the cellar like he was Dirty Harry or something would do nothing to calm the kid's nerves. The kid was already thinking of getting a gun. For sure now, he would obsess over it.

He walked quickly up the stairs, making sure this time that he turned all the lights off and shut the door tight. Mark stood at the entrance to the kitchen staring at him when he emerged from below. Jake's head tipped to the side, peering at Mark in return. "Did you go down there earlier? The light was on."

"No."

He blew out a long sigh. "Maybe your mom or Angela did. The light was on so I thought I'd check it out. Nothing there but spiders."

Footsteps on the upper set of stairs let him know that the women were ready. When Lydia rounded the newel post, her head jerked back seeing Mark and him just standing there outside the kitchen.

"I thought we'd check out that beach area before we head to town." She glanced behind her, "Angela? You coming too?"

But Angela was way ahead of her, handing her the down jacket. "I wouldn't miss it. I want to take a peek in the barn as well."

Mark had disappeared into the kitchen, and when he returned he was shoving his arms into his coat.

"We're ready if you are." Lydia smiled and her hand rose to rest on her son's shoulder.

"I'll just get my jacket." Jake slipped by them and went to the front door. As he lifted his coat from the hook he glanced down at the small table. The two sets of keys that he'd placed on the table were missing. But Lydia's purse still sat there.

When he slipped the jacket on, he looked down at the three of them. "Did you take the keys that I put on the table, here?"

Lydia shook her head. "No."

A quick glance at Angela and Mark showed a puzzled look while they shook their heads. But Mark had been downstairs before the women. Keys just didn't move themselves. And he'd need those keys to start the car.

"Are you sure you put them there? Check your pockets." Lydia turned, and her hand was on Mark's shoulder, nudging him to the back door.

Jake shoved his hands in his pockets but only found a gum wrapper and a ball of lint. He could have sworn he put those keys on the table. Mark. It had to be the kid who'd taken them. He'd have to get him alone and find out where he'd hidden them. What was with that kid? First he sees some mystery guy and then he hides the keys. If *that* wasn't a cry for attention he didn't know what was.

As he passed by the kitchen, he looked across the room to the window, doing a quick scan to the outside. But it wasn't the beach or water that caught his eye. The two sets of keys were littered over the kitchen table, the two silver rings sat next to them. Not only had the keys been moved but the little shit had taken them off the rings.

He stomped over and scooped the mess of keys and rings up. He couldn't stop the roll of his eyes when he shoved them into his pocket. It was a small thing, and perhaps for the boy's sake, it was best ignored. It wouldn't do to reward that kind of behavior. The kid was obviously acting out, but you could catch more flies with honey than vinegar. His grandmother had always said that, and so far, it worked most of the time.

When he stepped out into the fresh air, the sun was now hidden by a bank of gray clouds. Snow clouds. It was sure cold enough to snow. He flipped the buttons on his coat closed and then walked quickly to catch up with them. They were almost at the beach. He'd get a clear view from where the kid had stood and hopefully find some kind of explanation to reassure them. But after the key incident he was even more convinced that Mark was making it up.

THIRTEEN

Angela

Angela shoved the fuzzy mittens in her pockets. It had been a long afternoon running here and there getting groceries, and supplies, and she was tired. She gazed out the car window at fields of long grass, dead and leached of all color, while trees were black with only the odd, brown leaf stubbornly clinging.

They were still kind of crawling along the road. A quick glance out the front window revealed the yellow school bus they'd been trailing for the last few miles. The car came to a halt, right behind the bus. She looked out the window at a squat, brick bungalow. It was probably their closest neighbor from the looks of it. The driveway was long, easily accommodating the transport truck and an ATV parked at the end. Past the vehicles, at the very back of the driveway was a rusty, gray-metal shed with a door swaying from the track in the wind.

It was when the bus started again that the student who'd gotten off could be seen. A teenage girl with a blue hat slung low above a cascade of bronze curls, in a bulky parka and jeans. The girl turned her head peering at their car, a puzzled look in her eyes: she came to a standstill, openly gawking. She looked to be about the same age as Angela.

Jake broke the silence, "I guess we know where your bus stop is now."

The bus turned down another roadway, leaving the way clear. In the distance the tops of the trees outside her house, and the roof could be seen.

"You're joking, right? That's a hell of a hike to the bus stop." The fact that the bus had turned before getting to their driveway underscored the fact that Jake was probably right. Great. She'd freeze her ass off, while that girl she'd seen only had to walk the length of her driveway.

She looked across at Mark, hunched up close to the window in the backseat. He'd been quieter than usual—and for him that was saying something. He was probably still smarting from the embarrassment at the beach. There'd been no guy or bush that could ever be mistaken for a guy, and everyone knew it. For a moment she actually felt sorry for the little nerd. "Hey. You'll be glad we bought the playing cards and Monopoly. Who knows when we'll get the internet? Even Monopoly is better than nothing, right?"

Immediately, she could have kicked herself. She should have gotten Scrabble or Yahtzee. The last time they'd played Monopoly it had been a rainy day at Sanibel. Dad had cleaned their clocks in the four-hour marathon. If the memory stung her heart, Mark was sure to remember and feel bad too. She had to change tracks fast. "Did you go in the barn this morning? I didn't get a chance to."

He nodded. "Yeah. It kind of smells but there's a hayloft." He looked away for a moment. "If you go in there, wedge a rock at the door so you don't get locked in."

Beside Mark, a few flakes of snow brushed the window. She hit the button next to her and when the window slid lower, she thrust her bare hand out to catch some flakes. She'd seen pictures of snow falling but here she was, now experiencing it for the first time. A few landed on her skin and immediately melted, leaving her with only a chill to mark their presence. She pulled her hand in and put the window back up.

"Now I'll bet you're glad we got those boots. They may be clunky but they'll keep you warm. You'd freeze in those sneakers." Mom turned and smiled at her. "This is kind of pretty, isn't it? The snowflakes are bigger than I expected."

Jake laughed, "The first snows are usually like this. Pretty, but by the end of the winter, trust me, you'll be sick of it." He wheeled the car into their driveway. "The plow does the main road here but you'll have to look after clearing your driveway. There're lots of small contractors to do that."

Angela tuned them out, already picturing a hot bath and getting the chill from her bones. It might be pretty outside, but it sure was cold. Would she ever get used to the freezing temperatures? She edged forward a bit, "Can you get the fireplace going? That house is frigid."

"Sure. There's a stack of wood at the other side of the barn. Maybe Mark can give me a hand bringing some in." Jake turned and smiled at her brother, "What do you say, buddy? Two hands make light work."

Angela looked over at Mark. If the logs were any size at all, he'd never be able to manage. And he looked as chilled to the bone as she was. "I'll help too. Maybe I'll peek in the barn before it gets too dark."

Mark shook his head. "It's okay. You help Mom with the groceries and I'll get the wood." His jaw clenched tight and he looked out the window.

Well that was that. If Mark wanted to prove a point, that this was some *guy* kind of thing, lugging wood, that was up to him. The hot bath was sounding better and better. Maybe she'd light some candles!

***

Ten minutes later, Angela poured bath salts under the gush of warm water filling the tub. She went down the hallway to her bedroom and shut the door. After shedding her clothes, she pulled her robe on and knotted the belt. With pajamas in hand she went back down the hall to the bathroom, tugging the sides tighter against the cool air. She paused for just a second, her hand on the door handle. Was someone in there? It was quiet, the sound of pouring water was gone.

Her knuckles tapped the door, "Anyone there?" God, she hoped it wasn't Jake using the bathroom. Family was one thing and while Jake was nice, kind of good-looking if you liked the rugged type, it wasn't the same.

The latch snicked and the door opened a few inches. She eased back expecting Jake or Mark to step out, but nothing happened. From the muffled sounds downstairs, Mom was busy putting groceries away so it wasn't her in there. After a few more beats she pushed the door wider only to see a wispy veil of mist from the hot bath in front of her. No one there. Still, her eyes narrowed and she looked past the cloudy mirror above the sink.

The tub was only a quarter way filled but the faucet had stopped running. Great. With the age of the house, she wouldn't be surprised if there was an air lock or the well had dried up. She bent, about to fiddle with the tap handle when she noticed it was in the off position. What the hell? Someone had come in, used the bathroom and turned the damned thing off? How annoying. She flipped the lever and it began filling again.

She turned and went back to the sink. She might as well brush her teeth and get that out of the way while she waited for the bath to fill. If that was Mark who did that, she'd give him a swat. With toothbrush loaded with paste in one hand, with the other she swiped at the mirror to clear the steam, with the cuff of her robe. Her head jerked back and she almost dropped the toothbrush. For just a micro-second there'd been a face in the mirror!

Her hand flew to her throat and she gasped. It was the same girl! The face she'd seen there the day before had appeared in the mirror! But there was nothing now. But she'd seen it. For sure, she'd seen it. How could that be? She forced herself to take a long breath. Yesterday, she'd been so tired anything could have been possible. But now? A cold shiver gripped her shoulders and the hair on her arms tingled high.

What the hell? That kind of thing didn't happen in real life—only in horror movies. But she'd seen it, right? A girl about her own age but with really dark hair.

Her heart pounded in her chest and she backed out of the bathroom slowly. "Mom?" But from the sounds below, her mother busy doing something in the kitchen, Mom hadn't heard her. She blinked a few times, staring down the stairwell.

Had she really seen a face? If Dad was here, he'd look for a plausible explanation. He wouldn't just jump to the conclusion it was a ghost or something weird like that. Mom would think she was tired or seeing things, some trick of the light. The noise of the tub filling finally made the decision for her. She had to turn it off before it overflowed and caused a bigger problem. She would be an adult, assess the situation to find a logical reason for the fleeting image. Yeah.

She crept back in and then darted over to turn the tap off. It would be so much easier if she hadn't seen that face yesterday. She could blame today on the steam, the bleary surface of the glass. She straightened and scanned the area above the tub, searching for any shadow or ripple in the smooth surface that could have been caught in the mirror, making it look like a face had been there. But there was only the satin surface of the ivory wall. Certainly nothing that could have caused the dark hair in the image she'd seen.

Her body was tight when she turned to the window. But only the snow, falling harder in the fading light showed. No hope of a bird or tree branch casting a shadow to cause what she'd seen. She risked another peek at the mirror but it reflected the room, nothing other than what you'd expect to see. Some of the steam had drifted out and the room seemed normal enough now.

There was no way she was going to run crying to her mother about some face that was no longer there. Mom had enough to worry about with Mark seeing strange guys on the beach. And let's face it. None of them were operating at full capacity right then. She was no expert on grief but maybe your mind went a little wonky with reality.

She shut the door and locked it. Pulling her shoulders back, she slipped the knot of her robe loose. This would probably be the fastest bath she ever took but it had to be done. No spooky imagining was going to make her do otherwise. Besides, after she thawed from the day's errands she'd feel calmer. There was probably some reasonable explanation and she'd find it.

FOURTEEN

Lydia

Lydia's shoulders drooped as she stood in the kitchen putting away groceries. She was alone now. There was no need to be strong for the kids, methodically marching through the stores to get everything organized.

Angela had shown more enthusiasm over the vehicle they bought than the person who would be actually driving it. She really didn't mind the fact it wouldn't be ready for a couple of days. Jake wouldn't leave them stranded. Another night or two with him checking things out, at least until she knew they were absolutely safe, was a relief in more ways than one.

When he left it would be just the three of them. The stark reality of life without Liam would descend like a hammer. She didn't want to admit it, but it was also comforting to have another adult around. And in his mid-to-late thirties, there was more common ground than if she'd been saddled with someone fresh out of whatever school the FBI graduated from. It was obvious he wasn't married anymore but the sensitivity he'd shown to the kids, showed an easy familiarity.

Maybe he had kids of his own and was missing them.

Her ears perked as she lifted a milk jug to put away. Had Angela just called for her? She left the milk on the counter and went to the door of the kitchen, cocking her head to listen. She heard nothing but the running of water filling the bath. She shuddered and rubbed her upper arms. Angela was right about the chill in the house. She shook her head realizing she didn't even know where the thermostat was. She'd have to get Jake to show her where it was.

Stepping back into the kitchen her eyes flashed wide in surprise. The milk jug was now on the kitchen table? She left it on the counter, next to the fridge. She huffed a fast sigh; she was so distracted by what'd happened that she couldn't remember even simple things.

No. She knew where she left the damn milk!

Didn't she? With another sigh she stepped to the table to grab it. She paused for a moment to watch the snow coming down, a wall of white that shifted and danced in the air. She couldn't even see the beach or the river anymore. Was this what they meant by a snow squall? Squall. What a strange word. It was mesmerizing though; watching it swirl and eddy in the low light shining from the kitchen.

She turned her head at the sound of the back door opening and the thuds of stamping feet at the entranceway. She watched as Mark walked past the kitchen, his arms laden with a few snowy logs. Jake was right on his heels, but he paused at the kitchen entry.

Snowflakes clustered on his eyelashes and beard growth when he smiled and jerked his head, signaling the counter next to the sink. "If you're pouring, I wouldn't mind a stiff drink to take the chill out of my bones."

She looked over to where he'd signaled, and her breath froze in her chest. Next to the sink was an amber bottle with a familiar white label. Jack Daniels Honey? Seeing the glass next to it, filled with ice cubes and the liquor, she gasped. She couldn't catch her breath.

Jack Daniels Honey had been Liam's drink! He'd have one

after dinner every night. But how—

Fighting the sudden dizzy spell that came over her, her mind scrambled, recalling the trip to town and coming home. She hadn't bought the bottle of Jack, let alone pour *a drink*! Where had it come from? It hadn't been there before. Hell, a bag of groceries was next to it! Groceries, she'd put there.

Jake's head edged forward, his eyes narrowed. "Are you okay?" His gaze flitted between Lydia and the half-empty bottle, while his voice was barely above a whisper, "How many drinks have you had?"

She gripped the handle of the fridge and glared at him, "None! I didn't pour that drink and I sure as hell didn't buy that bottle of liquor! I picked up wine today but not *that*." She turned her head, staring at the bottle for a few beats.

How in God's name, had it gotten there? There was only her and Angela in the house, and Angela was upstairs taking a bath! There was only the two of them. Hell, she'd even locked the front door when they'd come in. Old habits from living in the big city.

She turned back to Jake, taking a deep breath. "Did you buy that whisky? I know I didn't." One thing at a time to get to the bottom of this.

He shook his head while his face tightened, looking at her with a skeptical glint in his eye. Shit. It was obvious; he thought she was losing it. Still holding the wet logs in his arms he stepped closer, peering at her like a bug under a microscope. "Lydia. It's okay to have a drink. You've been through some—

"No!" She spun away from him and then lurched over to the counter. She grabbed the glass of Jack and just stood there for a moment fighting the tightness in her throat. This wasn't right. The insanity of finding an opened bottle of whisky was bad enough. But why did it have to be Jack Daniels Honey?

Angela. It had to be Angela. If not, she really was losing her mind. First the jug of milk on the table and now the bottle of Jack?

She took a deep breath and lifted the glass to take a long

swallow. The cool burning sensation was real, the welcome jolt bringing her back to reason. She'd ask Angela about the whisky when she finished her bath. Maybe her daughter had put that particular bottle there to give her comfort? Knowing it was Liam's drink? Somehow Angela had managed to buy it without anyone noticing. That had to be it.

Her mouth turned down in a frown. Some freaking town, willing to sell a bottle of hard liquor to a fifteen-year-old! She knew the minimum age was twenty-one in New York, just like in Florida!

She looked over to see Jake watching her with a steady gaze. There was no way she was getting into this with him. This was between her and her daughter. She took another glass from the cabinet and poured a stiff one for the agent. Her head tipped to the side and she shrugged, walking over to the fridge for ice. "Well, the bottle's here now, however it got here." Affecting a casual ease, she waved her hand, signaling for him to leave with the wood. "I'll bring this in. You've got your hands full."

"It had to be Angela." Jake let out a long sigh through pursed lips. "Kids." He adjusted the load of wood and left the room.

She stared at the bottle as she walked by. The other part of the mystery was why it was half gone if Angela had just bought it? Surely, if her under-aged daughter was smart enough to somehow get her hands on a bottle of whiskey, she'd be smart enough to water it down if she'd sneaked some? And for sure, Jake had noticed that too. There wasn't much that got by him.

Following Jake into the living room she saw Mark was on his knees in front of the fireplace breaking up the shoe boxes and tossing them onto the grate. He looked up with a smile. "This will warm things up. There's a big pile of wood out there. Maybe enough to get us through the winter."

Before she had a chance to say anything, Jake leaned over, tossing some small twigs on the pile of cardboard. He smiled, looking over at Mark, "Hate to break it to you, but that pile will be gone by Christmas if the weather keeps up like this...which of course it will." He threw some more twigs on and then reached into his coat pocket. Bending over, he handed Mark a lighter. "You do the honors, son."

When he straightened, she handed the glass of whiskey to him. She then leaned over, putting her hand on Mark's shoulder. "I can see a new job for you, Mark. Chief wood hauler and fire starter. Good job."

She deliberated for just a second whether to go upstairs to confront Angela or just wait for her to come down. "I'm going to throw a roast in the oven and get dinner started."

She left them tending the fire and she paused at the stairs, glancing up and seeing her daughter emerge from the bathroom, a cloud of steam trailing her. Yeah. She'd wait to chat with Angela later. The last thing she needed was her daughter going off the rails, sneaking booze and then maybe getting into drugs. It would be easy for her to throw in with the wrong kids at a new school and go astray.

She needed a drink. And drinking Liam's brand wasn't all that bad. If only he was there to share it. She gritted her teeth. She wasn't going there; if she did, she'd start bawling again.

FIFTEEN

Mark

Mark sat back on his haunches gazing at the curls of orange flame. Jake was beside him on the floor, sitting with his legs stretched and crossed while he sipped his drink. It didn't seem right somehow. Here was this guy making himself at home, getting drunk when he was supposed to be watching over them, keeping them safe. And what was with "son" business? He wasn't his father.

He'd put up with all the questions when they were getting the wood. Being polite even though he wanted to yell at Jake and tell him to shut up. He'd seen enough TV shows to know when he was being grilled. Jake didn't believe him that he'd seen that old guy. Somehow he'd convinced Mom and Angela to doubt what he'd told them as well. They'd see. In the meantime, he was going to keep his mouth shut about any other weird stuff.

His eyes narrowed when he looked over at Jake. He was as comfortable as can be, moving right in. "I didn't think you were allowed to drink when you're on duty."

Jake watched him over the rim of the glass and then spoke, "It's just one drink, buddy. Just enough to take the chill from my bones."

At the creak of the stair, they turned and saw Angela standing in the doorway. The fleecy robe parted slightly to reveal her plaid pajamas and her hair hung in wet strings when she bent over to warm her hands over the fire. She flashed a smile at Mark. "The fire's good, isn't it?"

Jake got to his feet and drained the glass of whiskey. "If you're done in the bathroom, Ange, I'm overdue for a shower." He set the glass on the table and walked over to the sofa, grabbing a small satchel. "You two can look after the fire, right?"

"We've got it." Angela squatted down and sat next to Mark, soaking up the heat like a cat.

When Jake's feet thudded on the stairs, Mark hissed at his sister. "*Ange*? You hate being called that. And he's calling me, *son*." He shook his head and grabbed the poker, giving the fire a stir. Maybe when they got the car, Jake would leave. With any luck that would be tomorrow.

Angela nudged him with her shoulder. "He means well. Ange and son are just his way of talking. I'll kind of miss having him around when he goes. You have to admit, it's safer having him around."

Mark huffed. "If you call pulling a gun on me, *safer*!" He let the poker drop onto the hearth with a clang. The way Jake had questioned him about the keys still rankled. It wasn't bad enough he didn't believe him about the guy, but to accuse him of taking the keys was just insulting...and not true.

Angela stared over at him. "Jake pulled a gun on you? What the hell? What were you doing?"

He rolled his eyes seeing the anger in hers. But he had to tell her the truth. "He was checking the cellar and I went downstairs. I surprised him or something. I'm lucky he didn't shoot me."

She swatted his arm. "Well jeeze, Mark! He's the freaking FBI! You don't sneak up on those guys. Not if you value your life. That was dumb."

It was the straw that broke the camel's back. His hand shot out, and he hit her back. Hard. He'd had more than enough of being called dumb, not even believed when he was telling the truth! "Shut up! It wasn't dumb. You're dumb! You're barely passing in school, *Ange*!"

She got one more cuff to the side of his head before she flounced off, muttering over her shoulder, "Nerd!" And then she was gone, probably telling Mom how mean he'd been to her. He got up and went over to the window, waiting for his mom to come flying in to give him shit.

The storm was still raging, and the wind had picked up, hurling the big flakes helter-skelter. They were lucky they'd gotten the wood in when they had. It would be hard to find the house from the barn in that storm, a sheet of white had descended with a vengeance.

Sudden darkness obliterated the white haze. A face pressed close to the glass.

Holy shit! The old man! The guy he'd seen that morning! His body froze. The old guy kept staring at him. Mark didn't dare breathe. The guy's eyes were dark and squinty, an angry sneer set in his curled lip. And then he moved away. Gone in an instant...silently. White flakes again shimmered in the air outside.

Mark gulped, feeling his heart thud fast in his chest. His breaths were shallow and quick while his knees threatened to give out.

Should he try to see where the guy had gone? But if the old guy's face suddenly appeared in the window again, he'd piss himself. He wasn't totally sure he hadn't already. The back door! Had that stupid agent locked it? He raced through the house until his fingers closed on the latch. He flipped it shut. Oh God. He panted. That had been close.

"Mark?"

When he spun around Mom was in the hall just outside the kitchen. "What are you doing?" Her head tipped to the side watching him closely. "You weren't going outside, were you?"

He shook his head instinctively. Should he tell her? None of them had believed him before. With the doors locked they were safe from whoever was outside. The guy was old, not likely to break the door down no matter how pissed off he looked. "N...no." He sucked in a breath, keeping his shaking hands at his sides, out of sight. "I was checking the door, that's all."

Mom just rolled her eyes and sighed. It was weird. Normally she could catch him out when he lied. He was having a hard time looking normal, gulping for air and trying to get his heart to stop thundering.

"Were you fighting with Angela?" Without waiting for him to answer she kept going, "I need you two to get along, Mark. This is hard enough without you guys being mean with each other."

Angela's head darted out beside her mother's arm, her eyes full of spite. "He started it."

Mom's hands rose like a traffic cop. "Stop!" She spun on Angela. "*You* go into the kitchen. I want to talk to you." Turning back to him, "*You* go tend to the fire! No more arguing! Got it?"

She looked like she was ready to blow her top. Now was definitely not the time to say anything about what he'd seen. They wouldn't believe him anyway. He stormed off to the living room, shutting the curtains before he sat down near the fire.

He didn't take his eyes from the windows for a second.

SIXTEEN

Jake

Jake hooked his jeans and shirt to the back of the door and then stepped into the shower. The hot water eased some of the cold tension out of his muscles and he leaned forward soaking his head before scooping a palm full of shampoo to slather his hair and body. Even though the water pressure was fine, the spray at his own place, set to needle-like jets was better. There was always something off about using another person's shower, let's face it.

He closed his eyes when suds drooled down his forehead, his fingers pushing soap into his ear canals. Then abruptly the water stopped. Shit! They must be running the sink or dishwasher. His skin prickled with goose bumps in the sudden chill. He scraped the soap from his face with his hands and leaned forward to fiddle with the tap handle. Even a slow drizzle would help rinse him off.

He jerked back at the sudden rush of water. The handle had flipped to the closed position! What the hell? His eyes opened wider as he turned the lever and the spray started once more. How had that handle shut off? He couldn't blame it on the age of the plumbing since the taps and faucet were pretty damn new. One of the things that the artist couple must have changed. Maybe some sort of screw was cross threaded or something that it wouldn't stay on. He'd check it later. In the meantime he held it in place and rinsed off with his other hand sloshing water on his head and body.

Yet, the others had all used the taps and they hadn't said a word about any malfunction. And for sure they would have. Especially Mark. It would be one more thing for him to make a fuss about to get attention. Angela didn't need to do that. That kid could land in a pile of shit and still come out smelling like a rose. People were always drawn to someone with her confidence. It didn't hurt that she was gorgeous, much like her mother. Mark must take after the father.

He finished the shower and then turned it off. He flipped the curtain wide and grabbed his towel, wiping it over his face and head. The bathroom sure didn't keep the heat. He stifled a shudder and then dried the rest of him. He was about to step out when the yawning door to his left made him pause. He'd shut that door! Damn it! Someone had come in when he was using the shower and left the damned door open. Nice! He didn't have to think too hard to know who that someone probably was—the little shit.

He shoved the door closed and smiled at the resounding bang. Hope that scared the hell out of the kid. A glance at the floor showed his clothes were kicked under the pedestal sink. They were probably full of dust now. He was going to change anyway, but that wasn't the point, was it? The end of this assignment couldn't come soon enough. The poor mother had her hands full with that kid.

He grabbed clean clothes from his bag and quickly got them on. Just one more thing. He turned to check the shower. He turned the tap on and off a few times to see if it would move on its own, but each time it stayed where he put it. He blew out a long breath through clenched teeth. The kid probably reached in and flipped the shower off. Shit, while he'd been showering in there!

He gave the tub a quick rinse, shoved his used clothes in the bag and left the room. When he reached the bottom stair, he peered in the room at the boy. The kid was hunched close to the fireplace, but staring at the front window. And it wasn't like there was much to see there with the curtains drawn tight. He was probably trying to hide his face, laughing at the trick he pulled.

He strode over and glared down at Mark, "Think that's funny, do you?"

Mark's eyes were like golf balls when he looked up. "What?"

He had to give the kid credit for the poker-faced, total innocence. "You know what. Don't worry, I won't tell your mom but don't try that trick again. Got it?"

Mark's face screwed up when he answered, "I have no idea what..." His face cleared, and he spat the next words, "You left the back door unlocked. Anyone could come right in. Nice job."

So that was how he was going to play it—deflect. Plus the punk was full of shit—he specifically remembered ensuring that the back door was locked when he brought in the firewood. Little shit. Jake took a deep breath. "Don't ever come in the bathroom when I'm using it. That's not funny." He tilted his head down at the boy. "It's kind of weird, you know."

The kid jerked back and his face looked like he was sucking lemons. "Eew! As if." He turned back to the fire and threw another log on, sending a shower of sparks high.

Whatever. Jake took his phone out and walked over to the sofa. He had calls to make. If the kid wanted to be like that, fine. When he powered up the phone, there was no signal. Great. The storm must be getting worse to knock the cell tower signal out. He was stuck here until it cleared.

He looked up, hearing Lydia and Angela talking in the kitchen. From the sounds of it, she was giving the kid shit about the bottle of whiskey.

At the fireplace, the boy was still silent, sulking as if he had any right to do that. Yeah, Lydia had her hands full all right. One kid lifting booze from the store and the other making up stories and playing tricks for attention.

He sighed. They'd all been through some serious shit. They

were here for the long haul, but not him. The sooner this babysitting detail ended the better. He was really the only functioning adult right then and he would be leaving as soon as she got the car.

He gave his head a shake. If he was the only adult in the place he could act more like one. Instead of fuming at the kid, maybe try to get him to talk or something. "Hey Mark. Do you know how to play Gin Rummy? How about a game while we're waiting for dinner?"

The boy turned and looked at him like he'd suggested running naked in the snow. "Shouldn't you do a check outside or something? You're supposed to be protecting us, right?"

It was all he could do to keep from rolling his eyes. The kid was still milking the story from that morning—seeing some old guy on the beach. He really was making it difficult to be nice. "I *am* protecting you. But we're not exactly under siege right now, not unless you count the storm. It's doing a pretty good job."

He got up and stretched before walking over to the window and peeking out. "Holy cow. There's at least four inches that's come down since we came home." He turned to Mark, still holding the curtain to the side. "You ever see so much snow as this, buddy? Take a look."

Mark's gaze flitted between the window and Jake. He looked like a scared rabbit. Finally he spoke, "That guy is still out there, y'know. I saw him when you were upstairs."

Jake let out a long, slow breath. There was no way he was going to take the bait, indulge the kid with going out into a freezing blizzard. The kid had been upstairs and that was that. "Well, we'll look for tracks tomorrow when the storm stops. If there's someone creeping around outside, we'll know then. How's that?"

But the kid's only response was a look every bit as icy as the wind outside. Jake cocked his head at the loud voices coming from the kitchen; things were plenty hot in there.

SEVENTEEN

Anglea

Angela leaned her butt against the counter and crossed her arms over her chest. She looked at the bottle of whiskey and her eyes narrowed. Was this for real? Mom was actually accusing her of putting that bottle of whiskey on the counter? She glared at her mother. "First off, I was with you almost every minute today. And second, even if I wasn't, how would I be able to buy liquor? I'm fifteen, Mom."

"I know you're fifteen! I was there when you were born!" Mom's hands snaked through her hair and fisted, like she was about to rip it out. Tears flooded her eyes.

"Mom. Listen to yourself! I had nothing to do with that bottle of whiskey." Angela stopped herself in time before blurting the rest of her thoughts. Mom was losing it. The strain of losing Dad and being yanked from their home was killing her. Hell, she wasn't the only one! But she'd be damned if she was going to add to Mom's stress.

Mom's hands dropped and she strode over to the counter, and grabbed the bottle. "This was your father's brand."

Angela's chest ached when she saw the tears roll down her mother's cheeks. Her lips quivered when she answered her mother, "I know that, Mom." The fact that it was Dad's drink just reinforced the fact that her mother had bought it. Maybe Mom slipped it into the cart when she'd left. The two of them were only separated for the few minutes when she went to drag Mark from the gaming section. But that would have been plenty of time for Mom to pick up the bottle on the sly.

A cold dread seeped into her bones. Was this lapse of memory temporary? Would she have to pick up the slack running the house? Shit! Life really sucked.

Watching her mother pour a glass to the brim with the liquor didn't help ease her worry. "Do you think you should have that, Mom? I mean we haven't even eaten yet. Dad used to wait till after dinner."

Her mother jerked around to face her, sloshing a little on her wrist. "Yes, I need a drink from the mystery bottle. Maybe it'll make me feel better."

Was this woman with the disheveled hair, eyes bloodshot from tears, no makeup, wearing jeans and a sweatshirt really her mother? And drinking like this? Mom didn't do this kind of thing, and she always looked done up like a fashion model. Everything was falling apart.

She took a deep breath. "Do you want me to get the vegetables ready? Make a salad?"

Mom downed a quarter of the glass and then set it down hard on the counter. "Angela. Where did the other half of this bottle go? Did you take it?" Her eyes closed and she sucked in a breath, "First you pilfer this bottle and then you sneak half the contents? Tell me the truth. No more lies."

Angela's mouth fell open. What was *wrong* with her? Accusing her like this, not even the slightest attempt to be reasonable. "I'm not lying!" She pushed past her mother and then spun around in the doorway, glaring, "Maybe *you* drank it Mom! Right after you...yes YOU!...bought it!" She raced down the hall and then flew up the stairs. To hell with Mom!

She slammed the door in her bedroom and threw herself on

the bed, giving in to the flood of tears. This time it wasn't just sadness, missing Dad. She should just leave. Leave them all. Mom was losing it, and Mark...well, he wouldn't miss her.

She cried harder. Yes, he would. Who would stick up for him at school? Shit! Shit! Shit!

And Mom couldn't do this alone. She could picture her father's face, the sadness and disappointment in her for even thinking it. She'd have to somehow stick it out. If not for them, for Daddy's sake.

But there was no way she was going down for dinner. Let Mom chew on that.

She stiffened at the light taps on her door. Mom better not accuse her of any more shit. An apology would hardly even cut it.

"Angela?" Damn, a little kid's voice. Mom sent Mark up and he's scared stiff of all this; he sounds like a baby!

"Go away!" The last thing she needed was Mark wheedling and trying to be nice. Couldn't they just leave her alone!

At the creak of the door opening, she sat up, grabbing the pillow to hurl at him. She looked over but there was no Mark, just the door opening slowly. The little shit had opened the door and then ran away! Anything to bug her! She jumped up from the bed and with two resounding steps forward, she slammed the door again. This time she pushed the handle, locking it.

Something in the edge of her vision moved. Her head spun around, but there was only the window, sheets of snow swirling in the wind, while the tree branch clawed at the glass. But that hadn't been it. No, it had been larger, like a person. The hair on her arms tingled high again. That girl in the mirror? Her heart thudded against her ribs and she looked around the room.

Everything went black. Oh my God! Her hand flew out, hitting the doorframe. Her fingers flailed along the wall. Where was the light switch? Finally she found it and flipped it a few times. Still the room was black as tar.

"Mom!" She went to open the door. But nothing happened.

The doorknob wouldn't move. Oh God! Wait. She'd locked it, that's all. She twisted again and heard it click, popping the lock open. She lurched out into more black. All the lights were out?

"Angela! Are you okay?" Her mother's yell from downstairs was a small bit of relief.

Angela stepped slowly, feeling her way with her foot before planting it on the floor. She started at the sound of the creak of the floorboard; it went straight through her like a knife. She took a breath, trying to make her voice normal, "What happened to the lights?"

"Probably the storm, but I'm going to check the breaker panel." Jake's voice came up the stairwell. A beam of light danced along the walls, enough that she could see the railing and stairs. "Come on down here. I'll need this light to go down to the cellar." He held his cell phone out, using its flashlight app.

She had a cell phone downstairs too; they could use it as a second light. She hurried down, her feet thudding quickly on the stairs. Mom's arm was around Mark holding him close. She reached for her hand and the three of them stood together, watching the beam of light and Jake go down the hall.

"Let's sit next to the fire." Mom nudged them before her heading into the living room. At least the fire provided some illumination.

Shit! If the storm had knocked the power out it would soon get cold in there. And no dinner. They squatted down on the floor, huddling close to the heat source. Angela noticed that there were only two logs left on the hearth. That wouldn't get them through the night.

Maybe they could leave and get a hotel room. There was no way she wanted to stay in a cold house with no power. Especially not after what had just happened upstairs. This house was starting to feel seriously creepy.

EIGHTEEN

Jake

Jake's cell phone lit the way down the hallway to the cellar door. This was the very last place he wanted to be, with all the spiders and creepy-crawly things down there. He hated any and all kinds of bugs. He flipped the light switch on his way by, so there'd be light when and *if* the main breaker had somehow tripped, and he could turn it back on. Highly unlikely but still, one could hope.

He crept slowly down the old stairs, keeping his hand on the handrail. He pointed the beam of light along the wall where he'd seen the electrical panel earlier. But it was hard to tell if the main breaker was in the on or off position.

He inched forward, about to take the next step when he got shoved from behind! Hard. He flailed down the stairs, grasping for the handrail but missing. He hit the cement pad at the bottom with a resounding thunk that knocked the wind out of him.

His phone had gone flying at the same time, landing with a clatter and going out. Damn! Now he was in complete darkness. He winced with pain as he got to his feet.

Damn it! The kid? He pushed him? He took a deep breath. That shove had come out of nowhere and was really strong. There was no way that puny kid could have possibly sent him flying like that! He was almost two hundred pounds for God's sake. Even Lydia and Angela wouldn't be able to manage it. It had to be a guy. The kid had said he'd seen that guy again.

Oh shit. Maybe he hadn't been lying.

He had to get the hell back upstairs! There was someone in the house! The drug cartel? Oh God. Pain once more arced in his shoulder when he slid his hand in his pocket to grab the lighter. He flicked it on as his other hand reached for his weapon. He'd find the phone later; it was probably busted up anyway.

The lighter's flame did little to pierce the darkness, but it was enough to see the next stair. He held his breath, listening. There wasn't a sound on the stairwell, no breathing or anything to indicate that whoever had pushed him was still there, but he couldn't take a chance. He'd be no good to anyone if he got broadsided again. Not breathing, and listening with all his might he went up the stairs slowly.

When he got to the upper landing he fumbled at the doorknob. He had left the damn thing open when he started down, but now it was shut. He twisted it, but it remained firm. Uh oh—they'd locked the door. Oh shit. They had the family!

He twisted, hunching lower and kicking the door with everything he had. The vibrations shuddered through his shins but still the door stayed shut. He gave it another kick and then another, winding up for another assault when it flew open.

"Jake! What the hell?" Lydia's shocked eyes were locked on the gun.

He pushed past her, shielding her with his body. "Get down!" he hissed at her. "Where are they?" His eyes tried hard to see into the kitchen and down the hall. Only dark shapes showed from the dim light of the fire in the other room—too small to be grown men.

"What? They're here?" She darted out and raced down the

hallway to her kids. “Oh my God! *Do* something!”

All he had was the damned lighter to see anything! They could be hiding anywhere!

But why were they hiding? There’d been plenty of time to snatch the family or even kill them while he’d been locked in the cellar. “Did you see anyone in the house?”

“No but—”

“That old guy!” Mark’s voice was high-pitched, nearly hysterical. “He’s still out there! He stared at me through the window!”

“Oh my God!” Lydia’s wasn’t much better.

“Stay together by the fire. Don’t move. I’ll check the house.” Damn it! The lighter was getting hot in his palm but he held it high slowly creeping into the kitchen.

“My cell phone is on the counter! It’s got a flashlight app too!”

He swung his arm to the right and sure enough Angela’s phone was next to the sink. He scooped it up, letting the lighter drop right after. He found the buttons and immediately was rewarded with a beam of light. He kept his gun high, shining the light around the room. But there wasn’t anything there. He made his way through the rest of the downstairs, each room revealing nothing more than the furniture.

When he left the empty room at the back and returned to the living room, he stared over at the three of them, huddled together in front of the fire. “Stay here. I’m going to...” He cocked his head, listening hard. There was something upstairs. A muffled, low sound thrummed from above. He put his finger over his lips signaling them to be quiet and made his way to the staircase. The sound got louder with each step.

He jumped when all the lights came on. He blinked his eyes at the sudden brightness and slipped the phone in his pocket. The lights blazing just confirmed the power outage was storm related.

But there was someone upstairs. The someone who had pushed him and then locked the door! But each step higher, was more and more puzzling. They were running water in the bathroom? His eyes narrowed. A diversion. He'd bust in the door and they'd jump him from behind. Ignoring the closed bathroom door he darted into Lydia's bedroom and then the boy's. Nothing. He peered into the small bedroom next to Lydia's. Again, clear.

They could only be in Angela's, if they weren't hiding in the bathroom. He tiptoed across the hallway, wincing from the squeak of the floorboards.

He inched into the open doorway and pointed the gun, scanning the room quickly. A glance into the closet came up empty. He left the room and went down the hall, opening the bathroom door and then stepping to the side, out of the line of fire. After a minute, listening hard for anything besides the water rushing into the tub, he edged out and swung around, his gun high, ready to fire. But again, nothing. He'd gone through the whole upstairs and come up empty. There was nowhere else to hide that he hadn't checked.

He went back to the bathroom, peering around before he stepped inside. Leaning over, he flipped the lever, shutting the water off. He stood watching the water, thinking hard. Who turned the water on? Could they have got out of the bathroom and raced down the stairs without him hearing? And what about Lydia and the kids? They would have yelled if they'd seen anyone.

What the hell kind of cat and mouse game was going on?

His shoulder still hurt from landing on the floor. Someone had definitely pushed him but where were they? He shook his head. It made no sense, but they had to be outside the house now. They sure as hell weren't inside! He leaned and yanked the plug up from the drain before leaving the room.

When he reached the bottom stair, Lydia stepped out of the living room. She leaned closer, whispering. "Did you find anything? What the hell is happening here?"

He pulled her arm so that they were closer to the kitchen out of earshot, "Look. Someone pushed me down the stairs and then locked the door to the cellar! If you didn't do that then maybe that old guy that Mark keeps seeing got in. But he's not here!"

"What was upstairs? It sounded like someone was running a bath! We haven't left the living room since the lights went out. What the hell is going on, Jake? Are we even *safe* here?" Lydia looked like she was ready to kill him or start crying.

"Let me check the outside. There's got to be footprints!" He ushered her to the front doorway and grabbed his jacket from the hook. "Lock the door behind me. Don't open it for anything. Got that?" He slipped the jacket on and then opened the door. He paused, seeing the pristine drifts of snow that had gathered on the front veranda. Even to the lump of white that was the vehicle, nothing marred the velvety surface of the banks of snow.

He stepped back inside and shut the door, locking it. When he turned, Lydia's face was screwed tight with worry. "They're not at the front of the house. No one's been anywhere near it." He left her where she stood and continued down the hall to the back door.

When he opened it and peered out at the snow, again it was smooth. Nothing had disturbed the blanket draped by Mother Nature. He took the cell phone out and shone the light out into the yard. Again no sign of footprints. An icy blast of wind hit his face and he stepped inside once more, locking the door. What the hell? No one outside and he'd checked every inch of the house.

By this time the kids had joined Lydia standing in the hallway staring at him. Angela was the first to break the silence. "There's something wrong here. I don't think there's any guys trying to break in. It's. This. House."

NINETEEN

Angela

Angela took a deep breath and rubbed her hands over her arms, trying to warm up. The way everyone was staring at her, their mouths hanging open would have been funny in any other situation. But not now.

"I think this house may be haunted." She didn't have to wait long to be shouted down. She'd expected Jake and Mom to protest and was ready for it. The thing that cinched it was the water running in the bathroom. That room was seriously creepy.

"That's crazy! Angela!" Mom shook her head and let out a long sigh.

Jake walked past them and hung his coat on the hook by the door. He slipped his gun into the holster at the back of his pants. "The house is old, Angela, but—"

"She's right!" Mark's face colored, masking the freckles in a pinkish hue. He continued, "I saw that old guy staring in the window. But you didn't see any footprints. And how did he just disappear from the beach?"

Angela's stomach fell to her knees. She'd thought the poor kid had been making it up. And now he was the only one on her side! She took a deep breath and let it all out in a rush. "I saw a face in the mirror. A girl with dark hair and then she was gone! She opened my bedroom door earlier and I saw her again!" Her heart raced reliving it in her mind.

"Why didn't you tell me?" Mom took a step closer, her hand rising to circle her shoulders but Angela batted it away.

She snarled at her mom. "You wouldn't have believed me! Hell, you accused me of stealing that whiskey and then drinking it!" Mom's eyes opened wider, as the knot of the mystery bottle appearing unraveled in her head. But even if a ghost or entity had put it there, why Jack Daniels Honey? Dad was dead and...

Jake walked by them again, his words thrown over his shoulder, "I don't know about any of this, but I need a stiff drink right now."

Mom shot a look and then followed Jake down the hall and disappeared in the kitchen. It was just Mark and her now. Angela's hand squeezed her brother's shoulder, "I'm sorry for calling you a nerd...and for not believing you about the old man."

He looked up at her and shrugged. "Did you really see a face in the mirror?" He stepped closer, so close that his shoulder pressed into her arm. The poor kid looked fascinated and petrified all at the same time.

She nodded quickly. "Yeah. She was about my age, and she looked sad, come to think of it." She tilted her head at Mark. "I wonder how she died."

Mark scoffed. "The old guy looked pissed as hell! And mean, *real mean*. He probably killed her. I'm lucky he didn't do something to me on the beach." His eyes narrowed, "But why did he stare at me through the window? He's a ghost, right? They can come through walls."

That wasn't a reassuring thought. "C'mon. Let's go ask Jake what he knows about this house. He said an artist couple renovated it."

THUD!

She jerked at the bang upstairs. Her feet trembled from the vibrations in the floor.

THUD!

Mark's hands flew, fingers clutching her arms. She stared up the stairwell, while her heart hammered against her ribs.

Jake dashed from the kitchen, "What the hell was that?" He turned his head looking up the stairs. In another second the gun was back in his hand.

Mom was right behind him. "Mark! Angela! Come into the kitchen. NOW!" She grabbed their arms hauling them down the hall past Jake.

Angela twisted out of her mother's grasp. "It's the ghost! A gun's not going to do much good against a ghost!" She jerked away from her mother.

"I'll check it out. Stay here!" Jake was gone followed by the sound of him racing up the stairs.

Mark tugged on Mom's arm and there were tears in his eyes. "Can we go home? I don't want to be here."

Angela huffed, folding her arms across her chest, glaring. "We *are* home! Some house they put us in! Hell House! Our neighbor's probably Freddy Kruger!"

"Shut up, Angela!" Mom glowered at her and her gaze darted to Mark and back again, "You're not helping!" She turned away, holding Mark close.

"This is bullshit! Jake's not going to find anything up there and he knows it! Why won't you just admit that this house is haunted? Just admit it! It is!" And here she'd been planning to investigate why the bath had stopped on its own and that face appearing in the mirror. It made sense now.

She looked over to her brother and sniffed. "Mark's right. We can't stay here. They've got to put us up in a hotel until they find something decent for us. Maybe a house in California. Somewhere warm."

At the grating sound next to her, she looked over. The bottle of whiskey shot across the counter and flew into her! Holy shit!

Her mouth fell open, her eyes bulging onto her cheeks, watching. It sat there almost defiantly on the countertop. She edged away and looked over where her mother stood. Mom's back was to her, her arms cradling Mark. "Mom?"

Angela stepped away from the counter. "Mom!" She grabbed her mother's shoulder.

"What? What now? Honestly—"

"Mom. That bottle of whiskey just moved. All on its own! The ghost! *It's in here*!" She kept backing away, letting her hand drop from Mom, staring at the bottle.

Her mother pulled back from Mark and looked down at the bottle. She looked over at Angela, her eyes getting wider. "You're sure?"

The bottle shot down the counter and landed with a crash on the floor.

Angela bumped into the stove and jerked back. "Oh yeah. I'm pretty sure the ghost is making a statement, Mom." God! That had actually happened!

Jake stepped into the kitchen. "Nothing upstairs. I couldn't even see anything that fell over to make that noise." He looked at Lydia and then over at Angela. "What? What's going on?"

Mark was the one to break the pregnant silence. "No stiff drink for you. The ghost just smashed the bottle of whiskey."

TWENTY

Lydia

Lydia stared at the glass shards of the bottle in a complete daze. If she hadn't seen it with her very own eyes—the bottle flying the rest of the way down the counter and smashing on the floor, she would never, in a million years believe it. But it had happened.

Her mouth snapped shut. If the house was haunted... She blinked a few times. Was she actually thinking that? There was no other explanation for what she'd seen. And it sure explained how the bottle had just appeared earlier. She had to stifle a nervous giggle. The ghost liked Liam's drink? Good taste for a ghost.

Her eyes narrowed and she spun around to face Jake. "What the fuck? You guys put us up in a house that's haunted?"

His hands rose stopping her in her tracks. "Wait a minute. Lydia. Listen to yourself. Ghosts? There's no such thing as ghosts. Once you're dead, you're dead. There's an explanation for all this even if it's not immediately apparent."

It was all she could do to stop herself from belting him!

Her teeth ground together and she hissed the next words. "Just because you didn't see that bottle slide across the counter on its own, doesn't mean it didn't happen. And we..." Her hand swept the air, indicating the kids, "...we didn't do it. I know you think we did, but we didn't."

Her eyes narrowed and she stepped closer, "What about the noise upstairs just now? What caused that? Or the water running in the tub all on its own? Hell, you were even pushed down the cellar steps! Got a reasonable explanation for *that*, Mr. FBI?"

He couldn't look her in the eye when he replied, "No. Not all of it. The thumps could have been a tree limb coming down in the storm. You have to admit, that might be the cause. As for the other things..." He shook his head and sighed, "I'm not ready to just accept that it's caused by ghosts. And neither should you." He looked around at all of them. "Let's just sit down, try to stay calm, and figure this out."

Angela weighed in, "You stay calm! Knock yourself out trying to puzzle through this. The fucking place—

"Angela! Don't swear!" It was bad enough that she'd used the F-bomb, let alone her daughter.

"Why? You just did! Mom, let's leave. If he won't drive us, we'll take his car. Let him stay here to "figure it out." Please Mom. Mark's scared, and so am I." Angela rubbed her hands over her arms and shivered.

Seeing the look on both their faces was a knife to her heart. This shouldn't be happening! They were all innocent. The horror of their dad's death wasn't enough? This had to happen too? She looked up at Jake. "Well? Are you going to take us to a hotel or not?"

He looked around, shaking his head. "Look. Everyone settle down for a minute and think this through. In case you haven't noticed, it's a blizzard outside. It's probably more dangerous to be out there on the roads, than here." He looked at each of them and blew a long breath through pursed lips. "Tell you what. If you still want to leave after we've had dinner, I'll take you." He rolled his eyes and stepped over to the doorway. "I'll get my phone from downstairs and check the road situation. Maybe the plows are out. That's the best I can do right now."

Lydia watched him leave and then turned to her kids. "We're definitely leaving here as soon as we can. But..." She hated finishing the next part, "but if worse comes to worse, we managed last night all right. We can do one more night. He's probably right about driving conditions." Even though she agreed with the kids about leaving, she couldn't take a chance getting into a car wreck, maybe getting them killed. They'd manage somehow to get through one more night.

Angela's head fell to the side, "Seriously, Mom? You're taking Jake's side? This sucks."

She grit her teeth, trying not to lash out. But someone had to be the parent here and since she was the only one... "I'm not taking his side, honey. Let's not argue. If I'm on anyone's side, it's yours and Mark's, not some guy we don't even really know." She forced a smile, "We'll get through this. Now, you two can help me clean up that mess over there and get vegetables ready for dinner."

Mark tugged his sister's sleeve. "He said we can maybe leave after dinner. Let's get this over with."

Angela did a theatrical eye roll but rummaged in the pantry for a broom and dustpan, muttering, "This is not over. We're outta here after we eat."

Lydia walked over to the stove and opened the oven door. The smell of the roasting beef wafted up, but instead of the hunger she should have been feeling, the thought of eating was repugnant. She felt like Angela, going through the motions until they could get the hell out of there.

And why was Jake taking so long getting his cell phone? Who knew when the next thing would happen and she wouldn't mind the company of another adult. Even one so pigheaded as him. For God's sake, something had pushed the guy down the stairs! What would it take to convince him?

She got the vegetables out of the crisper and set them on the counter. Angela and Mark were quiet sweeping the glass and mopping up the puddle of whiskey. None of them would admit it, but they were all on pins and needles waiting for the next thing to happen.

Mark sidled up to her after dumping the glass in the trash. "Mom? I have to go to the bathroom."

She looked down at him. Her eleven-year-old son was afraid to go to the bathroom on his own. This is what the house had done to them. She wiped her hands with a paper towel and then nodded.

Angela's eyes flashed wide, stepping over to them. "I'm not staying down here alone. I'm coming with you." She silenced Mark with a look. "Don't worry, I won't come inside but no way am I staying down here."

Great. They were now all attached at the hip, afraid to be alone. Lydia sighed. "Let's go."

Mark looked up at her. "What about Jake?"

"To hell with him. He's on his own." She imitated the agent, deepening her voice, "There's no such thing as ghosts. Let's all remain calm."

Mark smiled and even Angela laughed a little. Shit. It was either laugh or cry. They'd all done enough crying for the time being.

She took Mark's hand and even Angela didn't pull back when she reached for hers. The floorboards creaked under their feet as they filed down the hall and then up the stairs. She looked up, past the bathroom door and along the dim hallway. Angela had seen a ghost girl, and Mark—that old man. But other than the bottle, she'd seen nothing. And that was A-OK with her.

Liam, if you're up there in heaven, send a little help. It's hell down here. Her forehead tightened. Maybe he was around. Why else would the whiskey be Jack Daniels Honey? Had that been a sign he was watching over them? It was a small comfort to think so.

She stepped forward and dropped their hands, signaling for them to stay put. The door opened at the touch of her fingers and she flipped the light on. The room was cool on her skin but other than that there was nothing out of order. She turned slowly and looked in the mirror. Still nothing but her own reflection. She turned and stepped out. "It's okay, Mark. We'll be right outside the door."

She watched her son walk in and their eyes met before he shut the door. Angela touched her arm and she nearly jumped out of her skin.

"Sorry." Angela took a deep breath, "Do you think I should get dressed? I mean, we're probably going to leave after dinner."

"Sure. It's chilly in this house so even if we stay, it can't hurt, right?" She glanced down the long hallway and then at her daughter. "I'll be right here. Go on."

Angela crept slowly down the hall and pushed at her door, peeking inside. She looked over at her mother and entered the room, making damn sure to leave the door open. Lydia took her eyes away from her daughter long enough to glance into her own bedroom. Should she get anything? Maybe a sweater?

THUD! It came from Angela's room!

"Angela!" She gasped and raced down the hall. Inside the room, her daughter was frozen to the spot, staring at the bed. She was in her jeans but the sweatshirt only half on.

Angela turned and her voice was like she was nine again, hardly more than a squeak, "The bed, Mommy. It went all up in the air and then...then it fell dowwwnnn!" She raced over and clutched Lydia's arm.

Oh my God! The ghosts were attacking the beds; that explained the earlier thuds. Holding on to her daughter, they slowly backed out of the room. They both jumped when the door slammed shut right in front of them. She yanked her daughter down the hall just as Mark emerged from the bathroom.

His eyes were wide. "What was that?"

Instead of answering, she grabbed his hand and they all stumbled down the stairs. Jake was at the bottom holding some old picture in his hand. "What happened? What was that noise?"

She raced by him, holding her kids' hands. "The bed! It just rose in the air and then slammed down. Angela's room." They went into the kitchen and she stopped, gasping for air. That was it. They were definitely leaving. If she had to bang the FBI agent over the head and steal his keys...they were out of there.

TWENTY ONE

Jake

Jake stood holding the old picture as Lydia and the kids flew past him to the kitchen. He decided he didn't need to go upstairs to check on the noise. Lydia had been pretty emphatic that it was the bed, and he was ready to give her some credence. It was the same reverberating bang that had happened earlier. With what he'd found in the cellar he wasn't even sure now that Lydia was wrong. Or Angela.

He held the picture higher and once more checked the back of it. In carefully scripted handwriting was written:

"Hawkins family, November 24, 1931. From left to right, Charles, his wife, Daisy, daughter, Nancy, and son, Jeremiah."

The fact that today was November 24th, wasn't lost on him. Finding it right out in the open after being down there a few times was beyond weird. It had been right next to his smashed cell phone, like he was meant to see it.

Like it was planted there.

Oh God. Too many creepy things had happened for him to dismiss all of this out of hand, even though every atom in his body ached for him to deny it. Hell, he was educated with a law degree! Maybe it wasn't ivy league but it was still a damn law degree! He'd even passed the damn bar!

He stood there silently as a scene from the week before played out in his mind. He'd had to be here when the van with all the furniture and appliances showed up. The delivery guy, an older man in his sixties had acted kind of suspicious, looking over his shoulder continually. After the third trip into the house, he braced the guy, grabbing him and shoving him against the wall. You couldn't be too careful when it came to the Witness Protection Program.

"What's with you? You casing the joint or something? You're always looking around, checking things out like you're sizing up the place!"

The guy stared at him wide-eyed, his mouth hanging open. This clown wasn't shifty—this guy was scared. And his answer confirmed it. "You don't know about this place?" The guy's head swiveled from side to side watching the walls and ceiling. "The fucking place is haunted, man!" Then he fixed his eyes back on Jake, "But you're not from around here, are you?"

"So what if I'm not? What's your point, bubba?"

The guy took a deep breath and continued, it all coming out in a rush. By the time the asshole was finished, Jake wished that he hadn't grilled him. "A guy that lived here killed his whole family and then he killed himself!

Jake rolled his eyes. "Oh come on!"

The deliveryman grabbed his arm. "No! It's the truth! Ask anyone who's from around here!" He glanced around the room again. "That's how come I know you ain't from the North Country." He looked back at Jake with a touch of scorn in his eyes. "Anyway, it happened back in the '30s, during Prohibition, and the guy, his name was Hawkins, he was a preacher at the church down the road. But they found all kinds of liquor in the barn out back!" The guy shuddered and looked up the staircase. "My granddaddy told me they found the kids still in their beds. He'd taken an ax to them, and they was all chopped up like firewood!" He shuddered again and pointed a finger at the stairs. "Right up there! They found the wife in the kitchen. The old guy, Hawkins, blew his head clean off with a shotgun."

Jake stared at the guy. "Yeah. Riiight."

"It's the damn truth, mister." The delivery guy stood up straight, taking on an air of indignation. "My granddaddy was on the police force. It was an awful mess it was."

Jake had only half listened at the time. It wasn't the first time he'd heard local yarns like that. But now, he held the evidence in his hand. There *had* been a family named Hawkins who'd lived there. And apparently some of them had never left.

"Jake!" Lydia stood in front of him.

He jumped a bit. He'd been so lost in his memory that he hadn't heard her come out of the kitchen. "What?" She looked mad as hell and scared. More scared than that delivery guy, for sure.

"Where's your cell phone? Did you check the weather and the roads?" She looked down at his hand holding the picture. "What's that?

God. Okay, she was scared, but she...hell, all of them were getting on his nerves. He took a breath to keep from lashing out at her. "The cell phone is broken." He lifted the picture. "I found this in the cellar."

By this time Angela and Mark had crept forward, peeking from behind their mother. Angela reached forward and grabbed the picture, "That's her! That's the girl I saw in the mirror!"

Mark had jerked over to her side, standing on his tiptoes and pointing at the old man in the photo. "That's the guy! He's younger, but I'd recognize that mean old face anywhere!"

Three sets of eyes stared at him. There was no way he was going to repeat the story the delivery guy had told him. They were scared enough. "I found this in the cellar. I think they used to live here."

Angela huffed, "They still do!" She looked into his eyes, challenging him, "*Now* do you believe us? We've got to get out of here!"

He stood weighing the risk of leaving. The Toyota was all-wheel drive. If he took it easy they might be able to make it to the main highway. The plows might even have been through. He looked at each of them in turn. They were scared as hell. Truth be told he wasn't all that crazy about staying either, not after finding the picture. They were counting on him to keep them safe, and for them the storm outside was the lesser of two evils.

He propped the picture against the stair railing and then took Angela's phone from his pocket. He read the words "No Signal." Damn. So much for checking the road conditions. He handed it over to her. "The storm has knocked everything out." That wasn't a good sign. He reached for his jacket. "Give me a few minutes to sweep the snow from the car and get it warmed up."

Lydia let out a sigh of relief. "Do you need help with that?"

"No. Get whatever you need for tonight." He stepped out into the snow, cursing the fact that his shoes did a piss-poor job of keeping his feet warm. They'd barely thawed from the trip to the barn to get wood and here he was outside, wading through a foot of the white shit again. Damn storm came out of nowhere. When he packed for this assignment the forecast was for clear skies till next week!

As he neared the vehicle the snow was past his knees, piled high by the whirling wind. He reached for his gloves in his pockets and then flipped the collar of his coat higher. Still the snow managed to get inside, freezing his neck as it melted. He unlocked the car and then got inside, starting the engine.

He got out and went around to the back, kicking the snow from around the exhaust before lifting the trunk to get the snow brush and scraper. He glanced down the laneway, barely able to see the path in the blinding flurries. Navigating the long driveway was going to be tricky. He flung the snow from the roof and windshield and looked up when a shadow crossed the outside light over the door.

Lydia and the two kids trudged toward him, kicking up

sprays of snow until they got into the car. The defroster had the windshield clear and had started to warm the car by the time he got in. All of them stayed silent as he threw the car into reverse. It might take a few tries back and forth but he had to get turned around to tackle the driveway head on.

He twisted in the driver's seat, trying to see how much room he had before he hit a tree. He pressed the gas pedal and the vehicle lumbered slowly through the drift of snow behind them. But at least it was moving. He eased to a stop. So far, so good.

Holding down the brake pedal, he started to spin the wheel in the opposite direction. What the hell? He felt the rear of the car lurch to the left and begin fishtailing out behind them. He shoved down harder onto the brake pedal, but with a relentless momentum the back of the car continued its path! He watched through the back window as the world slid by to the edge of the driveway.

Shit! They're going to go down! He put the car in drive and punched the accelerator, but it was no use. The back of the car slid down the embankment, hitting a maple tree with a crunching thud.

What the hell? It was like the rear had been broadsided and shoved off the road! Even if there'd been ice and the car hit it, they wouldn't have ended up in the ditch. Not from a standing stop.

From the front passenger seat, Lydia stared open-mouthed. Finally she said, "What happened? You drove into a tree." She glanced back at her children and turned to him again. "Can we drive out of it?"

He sat watching the back of the car and the snow-covered tree. No damn way that should have happened! He'd driven in snow lots of times, but never in all his experience had something remotely like this ever occurred. From a complete stop, the car had slid to the side and dropped!

He turned and looked at the house, his gaze rising to see the two windows over the front veranda like dark eyes peering down at him. The house. He couldn't explain why, but knew in his heart that the house had shoved the car off the driveway. His jaw tightened and he pressed the accelerator silently urging it forward. But nothing happened except snow flying up and hitting the wheel wells. The car was well and truly stuck. And it had nothing to do with his driving. He didn't want to think of what had done this to them. For sure, he wasn't about to let that cat out of the bag and frighten Lydia and the kids anymore than they already were.

He turned to her, and his hand twisted the key, shutting down the engine. "That's it. The car won't budge. It'll take a tow truck to get it out of the ditch."

Her face tightened into a knot. "I thought you knew how to drive in the snow. How the hell did you manage this?" She huffed a sharp sigh. "We can't even call for help."

Angela leaned forward, "We can just stay here in the car. We don't have to go back in there."

His jaw tightened and his words were low and even, "We can't do that. The snow isn't stopping and we'll freeze out here. And before you tell me to keep the vehicle running, that's not a safe option, not with the risk of snow blocking the exhaust."

Angela wasn't giving up. "What about walking? We can get out to the main road and go to the next house down. If nothing else we can probably call for help from there."

He spun around so fast, she jerked back. "Are you nuts? Visibility is zero in case you haven't noticed! You could go twenty feet and get completely lost! You'd freeze to death!" He turned around and took a deep breath. "There's nothing else but to stick it out for the night." He opened his door and got out. If he stayed in the vehicle one more minute, he was going to blow a gasket.

Like it or not they were stuck there.

TWENTY TWO

Mark

When mark opened his door, he had to really push. When it finally plowed through the wall of white, he slipped out, ending up waist high in snow. Oh shit. He tried to move his leg forward but it was trapped in the freezing bulk. He looked over at his mother but she wasn't doing much better. But she was on higher ground.

"Help! I can't move!" He reached forward, squirming and trying his best to get free. It was like quicksand but a whole lot colder. Some of the snow rubbed against his stomach where his jacket and shirt had ridden up.

"Hang on!" Mom leaned over and managed to grasp his hand. "Shit!" When she tugged, his mitt came away in her hand. "Can you roll forward and lift your legs?"

"What? You mean like try to swim in it?"

She nodded. "That's the only way out, I think."

His eyes squinted against the snow whirling and fell forward, getting a face full of it. But wriggling and twisting side to side like some kind of snake, he managed to free his legs.

Angela appeared beside Mom, and the two of them reached out and dragged him forward. At the top of the embankment, they pulled him to his feet, and the snow was up just over his knees. But at least he could move.

The three of them slogged their way back up the steps of the veranda. He glared at the front door where the agent had just gone through. Nice of the guy to stick around to help, all right.

The shiver rolling down his spine had nothing to do with the cold biting his face and hands. The house. They had tried to escape and had failed. It was like the house wouldn't let them go. It wasn't through with them yet. He looked up at Mom and Angela. From the tight look in their eyes, they were feeling the same.

Mom stepped past him and opened the door; she stepped inside, stamping her feet to get the snow off. The sound echoed in the silent house. Mark looked around and up the staircase, half expecting that old man or Angela's girl to come flying down.

When Jake came out of the living room, he still had his coat on. "I just put the last log on the fire. I'm going out to the barn to get some more."

Mom's mouth fell, gaping at him, "You're not! We don't need more wood." She slipped her coat off and shook the snow from it. "We can put the thermostat up. You're nuts to go back out in that if you don't have to."

"If the power goes out again, we'll need the fireplace." He started off down the hallway, "Just a few armfuls to make sure we can get through the night."

Mark looked up at his mother and she shot back a look, shaking her head. Good. He didn't want to go out there again.

Angela startled him when she called, "Wait up. I'll help you." She walked down the hallway ignoring Mom's pleas for her to stay. She turned her head. "If two of us go, it's just one trip."

Mom rolled her eyes and then helped him out of his coat. "We might as well turn the oven on again Mark. We haven't eaten since lunch. How about a hot chocolate to start with?"

Was she serious? They were spending the night in a haunted house and she was talking about eating? And hot chocolate? But he could see from the lines in her forehead, she was just doing this to be strong for him. "It's okay, Mom. As long as we're together, we'll be all right." He wasn't sure if he was trying to reassure her or himself.

Her eyes glistened while her face grew even tighter like she was going to break down crying any minute. "You're right. This is frightening but that's all it is; it's just scary, right? We stick together like glue and we'll be fine. It's just one night. This snowstorm has to stop sometime soon."

She straightened, and her hand rested on his shoulder walking down the hall to the kitchen. She walked over to the stove and paused. "I turned that off before we left. Now it's back on." She shook her head and even laughed. "The ghost. Pretty thoughtful, wouldn't you say?" She smiled down at him.

He grinned, meeting her eyes, "Think the ghost will make some hot chocolate?" If Mom could make light of this, then he could be brave along with her. But still he looked around the room, waiting.

Mom opened the fridge. When she turned she had the bottle of wine and the milk in her hand, giving the door a bump with her hip to shut it. "The hot chocolate packages are in that cupboard," she said, pointing with her chin.

He opened the door and then jerked back, gasping. There was a dead rat on the shelf. In stunned silence he watched as the cupboard door swayed; it almost closed by itself, then slowly opened fully before slamming shut with a sharp bang. "Mom!" He jumped and raced over to his mother.

As they stood there, his arms around her waist, trying to bury his face in her stomach, the cupboard door opened and slammed shut at least a dozen more times. He jerked as the thud of each slam went straight through him and he snuggled closer into his mother. '*Make it stop! Please make it stop*!' was a mantra in his head.

When it finally did, the silence was deafening. Whatever

was in that house, that mean old man didn't like them poking fun at it. And it had killed that rat. There'd been a puddle of blood next to its mouth, and its body was all twisted.

"Mom?" He looked up at her.

She took a deep breath, and when she spoke her words were hesitant, "It's...It's just...noise, Mark. You're okay. I'm okay."

"But it isn't. It killed a rat and left it for us. It's a warning. If it could kill a rat, it could hurt us, too!" In his mind's eye he saw the evil leer on the old man's face while he twisted the rat, snapping its neck. That old man wanted to hurt them too! If not worse!

Mom set the milk and wine on the counter and squatted down, taking him in her arms. He wanted to believe she could protect him but deep down he knew they were helpless. Even that FBI guy wouldn't be able to stop the bad things in that house.

The back door opened and the stomping of his sister and Jake's feet filled the air. He pulled away from his mother and rushed to the hallway. "It's still here. It killed a rat and then banged the cabinet door open and shut again and again!"

Angela dropped her logs and rushed over to him, grabbing his shoulders. "Are you all right?" Her eyes were wide, looking over his face and then trailing over his body. When Mom came out from the kitchen, Angela let out a long, slow breath.

Jake stood looking down at him, snow falling from the pile of wood in his arms. "I'll look after getting rid of the rat. It's just a rat. Old farmhouses have them." He headed into the living room to dump the logs.

Mark's eyes narrowed staring after him. Easy for him to say. He hadn't seen the misshapen, tortured creature yet. Why did the guy have to act so tough? Not a word about what he and his mom had just gone through. Just matter of fact, "I'll look after getting rid of the rat." Well, if he was all that smart and tough why couldn't he protect them from whatever the hell was in that house?

One thing he'd learned though. No more joking around

about the ghost. This was no laughing matter.

Angela slipped her jacket off and herded them into the kitchen. "You guys sit down." She looked at their mother, "You look like you could use a glass of wine." She made a wan smile. "Actually so does Mark, but he'll have to settle for milk."

As she set the stuff on the kitchen table she said, "We almost got lost going out to the barn. Shit, that's crazy outside." She turned to go back to the counter.

"It's crazy in here, too," Mark replied.

TWENTY THREE

Angela

Angela shrugged out of her coat and stood staring at her mother and Mark. Any question of walking away in this snowstorm vanished after the trek to the barn for firewood. If not for Jake breaking through the drifts, waist high in spots, she wouldn't have made it. There was no way Mark or Mom could do it. The snow that looked so pretty that afternoon was now claustrophobic; it was holding them prisoners in this hellhole.

She took a seat at the table. "What about tonight? I mean, we can't possibly sleep upstairs."

Mark chimed in right away, "I'm not sleeping up there."

Mom nodded, gazing into the wine glass in her hand. "No. I agree. But we'll be warmer and more apt to sleep if we have the comforters and pillows."

Angela's heart kicked up a notch, and she blurted, "I'm not going up there! Jake can get our bedding! He's the one who—"

"The one who *what?*" Jake stepped into the kitchen. His eyes were hard glaring at them. "It's one night, okay? There's not much we can do about getting out of here." He grabbed a glass and poured some wine into it. "Finish what you were saying, Angela."

Her face heated at being caught out. But this was his fault. Her jaw tightened watching him. "You're the one who doesn't believe this place is haunted, that's what! We need you to go upstairs to get our bedding."

He walked over and stood staring at them silently for a minute or so. It looked like he was thinking hard about something. Finally he spoke, "I take it you've decided to camp out in the living room tonight."

Mark's voice was low when he ventured a suggestion, "We need to take turns sleeping and standing guard." He dropped his voice to a whisper. "Whatever this is, it's getting worse!"

He leaned closer to Mom before she weighed in and said, "We need to stay together." She looked up at Jake, "You said it yourself. If the power goes out we'll have the fireplace. We're staying downstairs tonight. Can you get the bedding or do I have to go up there? It's got to be one of us."

"No Mom." Mark clung to her, burying his face in her shoulder.

But Angela did one better. She grabbed her cell phone from her pocket and handed it to Jake, "Here. In case the power goes out when you're up there."

The resigned look on Jake's face showed that he knew he was outnumbered. He let out a long breath and took the phone, "Okay. Stay here. I'll be right back."

She couldn't resist, "We're not going anywhere. But don't worry, Jake. There's no such thing as ghosts."

His eyes narrowed, and he left the room. For a skeptic, he looked pretty nervous. She kind of felt bad for him, just a little. But it was thanks to his stupid organization, they were stuck in a creepy house. Still, he did try to be decent about going upstairs. She followed him from the living room and called out, "Hey. I'm not going up but I'll stand next to the stairs to keep a lookout for ya."

At the staircase her hands gripped the top of the newel post as she watched him ascend. That picture he'd found was on the floor beside her leg. She picked it up and flipped it over to read the writing on the back. That girl she'd seen. Her name had been Nancy.

She flipped the photo back over to look at Nancy and gasped. The picture had changed! She froze, staring at the figures in the photo. They were all covered in blood! Nancy smiled back, but with gaping, dripping wounds in her neck and arms. Blood oozed from her, across the glass and dripped down to the edge of the frame. Angela's heart skipped a beat and her knees went weak. Dropping the photo, she grabbed at the post as she sunk down onto the stairs.

Jake's feet thudded down steps, "What was that? Are you all right?"

She gaped up at him and turned her head to see her mother and Mark as they rushed to her. She couldn't speak. It was like being in a nightmare, where you tried to scream but nothing came out. Her hand shook when she pointed to the picture laying face down on the floor.

Jake pushed by her and reached for the picture brushing her mother's hand away. "I've got this!"

She couldn't look! He held it beside her and she shrank away, sinking to the stair, gulping for a breath. Oh my God! Would that picture ever leave her head? She could still see it...all the blood and horror. Even the son and mother in the picture were covered with blood. She looked down and red showed on her fingertips! Oh my God! Their blood!

"What is it?" Mom reached for her and pulled her in close. She stared at Jake holding the old frame.

"Never mind!" Jake almost knocked her off the stair as he brushed by her. He stormed into the living room and then the metal curtain covering the fire scraped. A small thud followed. "There!" Jake closed the fireplace shield and then came out. "It's gone! I burned it."

All the while, Angela cried staring at her hand smeared with blood.

Mom almost screamed, "Oh my God! You're hurt!" She

pulled her to her feet and down the hall to the kitchen.

Tears continued to roll down Angela's cheeks. That picture...The family had been murdered. But the father hadn't been butchered. Half of his head had been gone, like from a shotgun blast.

Ohmygodohmygodohmygod.

We're doomed.

TWENTY FOUR

Lydia

Lydia held Angela's hand under the stream of water. She peered at her fingers and palm but there was no cut—nothing to explain the blood that swirled in the basin and washed down the drain. She looked at Angela, still crying silently, her eyes and mouth both wide. A tiny runnel of spittle ran from the side of her mouth. The girl was in shock! She'd seen enough TV shows to know the symptoms. But what do you do to treat shock?

Warmth! You have to keep them warm. Keep the blood circulating. BLOOD! Like the blood on Angela's hand? Oh God. She heard Jake in the doorway and turned to him. "What the hell is going on? How did this happen? Could she have cut her hand on that picture?" This was insane.

He shook his head and his mouth opened like he was about to say something and then snapped shut. "Get her something to drink!"

She ignored him and turned to Mark, "Get her coat! We've got to keep her warm." She pulled Angela into her and her hands rubbed fast along her daughter's back. "It's okay, honey! You're okay." She kissed her daughter's temple while tears built up behind her eyes. Why was this happening?

Mark handed Angela's coat to her while Jake had a bottle of coke in his hand, offering it. She pulled back from her daughter. "Here honey. Put this on." Oh God. She had to lift Angela's hands and direct them into the sleeves. Angela had become a zombie! The last time she'd had to dress her daughter; Angela had been a baby. What the hell had happened to make her like this?

She tugged the jacket up over Angela's shoulders and then grabbed the front opening, giving it a firm shake. "Angela! Come on, honey! What's wrong?" Oh my God! She was white as a sheet and her mouth still gaped open. Lydia's hand rose and she slapped her daughter's cheek. "Angela! Snap out of it!"

"No Mom!" Mark grabbed her hand before she could strike Angela again.

"Lydia! Here. Let me." Jake held Angela's chin between his thumb and forefinger, tilting her head and placing the bottle of coke against her lips. "The sugar will help." But instead of swallowing, a brown drool rolled over Angela's chin. "Come on Ange, just a sip." He wiped the spit away with his finger and put the bottle against her lips once more.

Still, she was vacant, the liquid rolling over her lips. Jake handed the drink to Mark and then tapped Angela's cheeks quickly. "C'mon! Angela, it's okay. I know what you saw. It's not real though. You're safe! We're here with you."

Lydia stared at him. The picture. Angela had seen something horrible. It explained the catatonic reaction but not the blood. Whatever she'd seen had been bad enough that Jake had burned it immediately. Oh my God.

Angela's eyelids flickered and she blinked. They started to clear as she focused them. Oh, thank God! "Angela! It's okay honey! You're okay." She smiled and swiped the tears from her eyes, before her hands cupped her daughter's cheeks. She pulled her close and kissed her forehead, saying a silent prayer of thanks.

Mark tugged at Angela's arm. "What was it Angela? What did you see?"

Jake silenced Mark with a quick wave of his hand. "Never mind. It's gone now." He turned back to Lydia, "Let's get her into the living room. I'll pull the sofa over next to the fire. We've got to keep her warm and quiet." He put Angela's arm over his shoulder and lifted her. "Bring that drink, Mark."

Lydia took Mark's hand, following Jake and Angela from the room. When they were inside, the two of them shoved and pulled at the sofa, until it stretched directly in front of the hissing flames. Jake had barely set Angela down on it before Lydia was beside her daughter, cradling her in her arms. The kid was still quiet, although she'd looked at each of them. Whatever she'd seen had shocked her to the core.

Mark sidled close on Angela's other side. "Here Angela. Drink this. You'll feel better if you do." But the look in his eyes betrayed his words. His lip trembled showing that he was close to losing it as well.

Jake poked at the fire, making sure that the last corner of the photo caught in the fire. "We've got our coats. That'll have to do us tonight."

She looked up at him. Whatever he'd seen in that photo had traumatized Angela and made him a believer. That wasn't reassuring.

TWENTY FIVE

Jake

Jake pulled the armchair over and set it beside the fireplace, pushing it until the back was tucked tight to the wall. From that spot he'd be able to see across the room and into the other room, keeping an eye out for anything. And it was definitely *anything* when it came to that house. Whatever crazy shit was going on here, it had piled the car into the ditch and now the daughter was in shock.

He plopped down into the chair and looked over at them huddled on the sofa. No wonder Angela was traumatized. He'd almost shit himself when he saw the picture. It wasn't the gore. Hell, he'd seen lots of worse things than that. No. It was that the picture had *changed.* His blood ran cold, and he couldn't help the shiver that gripped his shoulders. Some of that blood had gotten on his fingertips but he'd wiped them clean before he went into the kitchen. Just the thought of it, made him want to wash his hands. But he couldn't wash away the image that lingered in his head.

Half the guy's head had been blown off! The wife and kids

were chopped up like minced meat. And in case he didn't think that was bad enough there'd been blood. Real blood, dripping from the photo, onto the frame and onto his hands. It was that blood that freaked the girl out. Caused by… a ghost, dammit. Yeah. Point taken. He glanced at his watch. Only a little past eleven.

This was going to be a long night.

The girl was still quiet, staring into the flames. Not a word had passed her lips. She hadn't even swallowed any of that coke. Oh God. She needed medical attention. Psychiatric help for sure, after going through this. He had to do something. "I'm going to put some soup on for her."

Lydia gaped at him like he had two heads. "We need to get out of here, and you're making *soup*?"

He shrugged. "Sorry. It's the best that I got right now." He pointed a finger at Angela. "She needs liquid and warmth."

He wanted to wash his hands as well; God only knows what was in that blood! He got to his feet and walked across the room, to glance outside. It had been too much to hope that the snow would have let up.

He peered up the staircase as he walked by. Nothing unusual. Just the dark space and the door to the bathroom hanging half open. In another few steps he was in the kitchen. He jerked back when a glance in the cabinet showed the dead rat. Yeah. He'd said he would take care of it. Shit. He inched forward, with his lips curled and picked it with two fingers by the tail. Oh man. Something had mauled it pretty good and he didn't want to think what that something was.

He turned to the back door but then shook his head. Screw it. He opened the cabinet under the sink and tossed it in the trash. He wasn't stepping a foot outside if he didn't have to.

Freaking pencil pushers in Washington. They'd bought this stupid house never questioning why they'd been able to get it so cheap? The locals knew though. He gave his head a small shake. What if Washington had heard the story about this place? It wouldn't have changed a damn thing; he hadn't believed the delivery guy, right? And it was highly unlikely the bureau would ever believe him if he told them this story. He'd be lucky not to get kicked out as a psycho.

He washed his hands pouring plenty of dish soap into his palm. No wonder that artist couple had just up and left even after sinking all that money into reno's. Who could blame them?

He found a can of chicken noodle soup and opened it. When it was in the microwave warming, he noticed the red stove light still on. He turned it off, shaking his head. There was no way anyone wanted to eat. But it was important to stay hydrated. He rummaged in the cabinets until he found a tray. He got a few cans of pop, glasses, and the bottle of wine. Lydia could probably use a stiff drink, 'cause he knew he sure needed one.

When the microwave beeped he grabbed the bowl of soup and set it on the tray. For good measure he grabbed a bag of chips and plopped it on top. The boy might appreciate some junk food. He paused for a moment remembering how he'd blamed Mark for the shower prank. The kid had been innocent. His lips twitched. He owed that kid an apology. He chewed his lip. Who was he kidding? He owed the boy a slew of apologies.

He went down the hall and crossed by the stairs to the living room. He could see their heads above the back of the sofa and hear the crackling fireplace. Breathing a sigh of relief he went over and stood next to Lydia. "Try to get some of this into her. Has she said anything?"

Lydia shook her head and took the bowl of soup and spoon. "Thanks."

Holding the tray in one hand, he tossed the bag of chips to Mark. "Here. Thought you might like something. I've got another soda for you too."

As he was about to set the tray on the floor by the chair, a thundering boom crashed above. And another. And another. His jaw tightened and he stood perfectly still. The banging continued. It was like the whole upstairs was caught in a maelstrom; with the crashing was so hard that he could feel it in his bones. The walls shook, and the can of soda on the tray danced across the surface. Jake stared at the ceiling, his hand automatically reaching behind him for his gun. The crashes kept going.

"Make it stop!" Mark screamed and his arms went round his sister.

Lydia dropped the soup bowl onto the tray and grasped her children. Mark was still screaming and Angela's eyes were so wide the whites showed! She began to tremble and shake as her mouth yawned open wide in a silent scream.

An icy shiver skittered up his spine, and he froze holding the gun in his clenched hand. He had to do something! He darted across the room and glared up the stairwell. "Stop it! For God's sake, *just stop*!"

The sound of breaking glass followed. But the thudding noises ceased. It was so quiet he could hear his heartbeat echoing in his ears. A cold draft settled on his shoulders as he peered up the set of stairs. Whatever was up there had smashed a window, letting icy air into the house. Even if the electrical power stayed on to keep the furnace going, it would be a losing battle to stay warm.

He took a deep breath and tucked his gun away. Fat lot of good a gun would do in this house. He turned around and called to Lydia, "I've got to lock the bedroom doors. It's the only way to keep the heat in." His gut tightened into a knot when he turned and looked up at the second floor railing. Like it or not, he had to go up there.

The loud creak of his foot on the stair sent his hackles high. His hand gripped the railing in case something tried to push him again, like in the cellar. There was no doubt that there was some entity lingering in the horrible old house. Just a few more steps and he'd be up there. His gaze flitted down the hall and then to Mark's bedroom on his right.

Bending at the waist, he looked into the bedroom. His breath froze tight in his chest. The bed was upended, leaning against the far wall. The chest of drawers lay flat on the floor, clothes spilling from the drawers that littered the room. A cyclone couldn't have done more damage. He flicked the lock on the knob and shut the door.

Standing in the frigid hallway he sucked in a deep breath. He had to get this done before he lost his nerve. He held his hands out in front of him to ward off any attacks as he crept to Lydia's room.

His mouth fell open, his gaze riveted to the massive oak frame of the queen-sized bed. It was completely flipped over, the mattress and bedding splayed underneath. What the hell could do that? Again clothes were strewn everywhere and the dresser lay on its side. But the window was intact, just like Mark's room had been. Shit. It had to be the girl's room where the glass had shattered.

He locked the door to Lydia's room and again crept slowly down the hallway. He checked the spare bedroom only to find the bed also on its side. He secured the door and took a deep breath. He knew it had to Angela's room where the window was smashed out. He could feel the cold draft.

Opening the door, he saw flakes of snow drifting onto the glass shards below the window. The steady wind whipped the lace curtains high. Even with the smashed window, the devastation in this room was minimal compared to the other two rooms. The dresser and night tables were undisturbed, the girl's belongings untouched. As he went back to the door, sudden movement on the bed caught his attention.

He ducked just in time to dodge a book flying past him and through the open doorway. When he straightened he gasped! A girl sat on the edge of the bed watching him with dark eyes. Her hair was black, hanging in strings over her sallow cheeks. Her hand rose, reaching for him and her head tipped back, her mouth open in a silent scream. In the dim light he could see a gaping gash in her neck. Arms outstretched, she rose from the bed.

Oh shit! He had to get out of there! He lurched into the hallway, yanking the door shut with a resounding bang! Gulping air, he kept his hand on the door handle holding it shut. Oh God. That had been the daughter! And that gash in her throat...The old man had almost taken her head off with that ax!

He spotted the book she'd thrown, laying against the wall. He bent to grab it and then raced down the hall to the stairs. Please God. Let the door keep her in there! If he ever saw that specter again he'd have a heart attack. His heart galloped, threatening to burst from his chest. He paused at the newel post, holding on and gasping for air.

"Jake? What's happening, Jake?" Lydia cried out from the living room.

Oh God. He had to get a grip. He couldn't tell them what he'd just seen, they'd totally freak out! Hell, he was freaked out. He looked at the book in his hand. There were flowers on the cover; the word "Diary" was embossed below that. He stared at it blankly. She wanted him to read it? *Now*?

He took a breath and huffed it out fast. Later. He'd look at it after they got out of this mess. *IF* they got out of there. He couldn't handle much more.

TWENTY SIX

Mark

Mark held Angela's hand in both of his—his big sister who always looked out for him despite their bickering. And now she was a zombie. He fought the tears threatening to spill out any second. It was up to him to take care of *her* now.

He looked over his shoulder when the thuds of Jake coming down resounded through the house. He watched the man take the stairs two at a time, thundering down to the main floor.

Mark gulped hard in a mouth that had gone bone dry. Whatever Jake had seen upstairs had scared the hell out of him. It looked like he was barely standing, hanging off the banister, panting for air.

Oh shit. The agent was an adult, and *he* was scared to death? What chance did Angela have...or him, for that matter? He looked over at his mom when she called out to the agent in a shrill voice. She was just hanging on with her fingernails.

Jake stumbled into the room. A sheen of sweat on his

forehead showed in the light above. His face was pale and his mouth hung loose, kind of like Angela's. Oh no. They'd counted on Jake and he was losing his shit. They were really screwed now!

He turned and stared into the flames of the fire. "Please Dad, if you're around and can help us, we need you," he said to himself. If only Dad was there. He took a deep breath, picturing his dad's face, the way he always encouraged him when other people had only sarcasm or taunts to throw at him. What would Dad do now? He reached for the bottle of soda and took a long haul, shutting out everything but his thoughts. There had to be a way to survive this nightmare.

Mom had said that this wasn't real, that this was scary but it hadn't hurt them. He looked over at his sister who was staring bug eyes at the fire. She wasn't physically hurt but fear...fear had zoned her out. When he looked at his mother, at the tears rolling down her cheeks, her forehead creased with dread, it was clear she could end up like Angela any minute.

Jake hadn't said two words since he'd come back from upstairs. It was getting to him too.

He took a deep breath. A really deep one, like right from his belly like he'd seen the yoga woman on TV do. In the few times he'd watched it, to see the women's boobs when they contorted into weird poses, the woman had always harped on about the breathing. Calming, cleansing breaths from your core. He sat still, closing his eyes and doing ten, deep, measured breaths.

When he opened his eyes again, he was surprised to feel calmer, his heart beating slower. It might not change the scary shit that was going in the house, but at least it made him feel a bit better. He didn't know how it worked, but he definitely felt calmer and more in control.

Just like in *Minecraft*.

Minecraft? There was something there. His face tightened as he tried to understand why that popped into his head. What about *Minecraft*? There was something he was missing.

Jake flopped into the chair by the fire and then stared at

Angela. "She's still the same?"

Mom held a spoonful in front of Angela's lips. "C'mon Angela. You need this. Everything's going to be all right." Her head turned to Jake and whispered, "What happened upstairs? Did you get the window shut?"

Jake nodded. "Every door is locked now."

Mark's eyes went wider watching the agent. It wasn't the scared look in the guy's eyes that was alarming. It was his voice, flat and robotic. At least his mother was pissed. That was better than Jake or Angela with their zoning out. That was a surefire way to be beaten. Beaten by that old man and Angela's girl ghost. The old man was scary but a *girl* ghost?

He took another deep breath for good measure and then spoke, "We have to stay calm. What's the opposite of being scared?" He peered at Jake and then his mother, ignoring the fact that they looked at him like he'd grown a set of wings or something. "Well? Come on. You should know this. I'm a kid, and I know the answer."

His mother gave up on spooning soup into Angela and set the bowl on the floor. She rolled her eyes and then sighed, looking at him. "The opposite of fear. I don't know, laughter? How well did that work out in the kitchen, sport?"

But Jake was watching him closely, even if his mother wasn't getting it. He took a breath, "Keeping our wits about us. Control. When you're in control you aren't scared. Is that what you're getting at Mark?"

He leaned forward and stirred the fire with the poker. "Yeah. Kinda. I keep thinking of *Minecraft*. I mean here's this scary house with ghosts and weird stuff. It's a creation. We're like the ghouls and monsters that have invaded it. The house was perfectly fine until we moved in to live here."

Mom continued to rub Angela's back but flashed a look at Jake, "Which we're not! I'll take a tent pitched under a bridge before I spend another night in this hellhole. Look at my daughter—"

"Mom! Stay with me here, will ya?" Mark shook his head and continued, "I'm not sure, but I think we need to fight back. Or if not fight back, at least defend ourselves."

Jake nodded and leaned forward, putting his elbows on his knees. "Not be victims. That's essentially what you're getting at. We go about doing stuff, like checking the breaker panel and they attack. We get freaked out. And look at what's happened to Angela."

Mark slumped back and turned to face his sister. They were talking about her like she was not even there. He tugged her hand, "Angela? We need you to talk to us. I know you saw something really bad, but it's not real. Whatever is in this house isn't alive. It's not like you or me." He grabbed her hand and pinched the flesh between her thumb and forefinger, twisting it until she jerked away.

He nudged her with his shoulder, "See! You're alive. You're here next to the fire! If you don't talk to me, I'll tell Mom you skipped school last week to spend the day with Adam Wilson. I saw you two sneaking off to the beach, holding hands and kissing. You'd changed into that skanky dress you're not allowed to wear and— "

"Shut up!" Angela swatted his arm, almost knocking him off the sofa.

"Angela!" Mom's hand rose, twisting his sister's head until she faced her. "Oh my God!" She hugged her as tears poured from her eyes. It was the first time he'd seen Mom smile in three days.

That swat had stung but still he couldn't stop the grin that spread on his face. He'd had to piss her off to get through, but it had worked!

Angela's eyes were narrow when she turned on him. "You little shit! Why'd you have to tell on me? You're always sneaking around, aren't you?"

He grabbed the bag of chips from the floor and tore them open. Pouring the chips over her head, seeing her get even madder felt sooooo good. Even the punch to his shoulder was nice. His sister was back.

"Stop it! You two, cut it out." Mom swiped a tear from her eye, and couldn't stop smiling.

Jake's head fell to the side and he shot Mark a thumbs-up. "That was pretty good, kid. Pretty smart."

But Mark didn't need the praise. It was good to have Angela with the living again. Things were looking like they might just get through this.

TWENTY SEVEN

Lydia

Lydia had never heard such beautiful words as the insults her kids hurled at each other. The spark was back in her daughter—Angela was herself again. The horror that she'd seen was still ingrained in her mind, but it no longer claimed her, making her the latest victim of this house. She gazed at her son. Mark had done it. He'd puzzled through this and been able to help his sister. Jake was right. He was a smart kid.

She turned, and her hand closed over Angela's wrist. "You should eat something or at least drink your Coke." When she leaned over to get the soda, she winced. She shouldn't have drank that wine. She had to pee but the thought of going upstairs to the bathroom was terrifying, even if they'd somehow got their second wind. She'd rather take her chances going out in the blizzard, squatting in a snow bank. No. This was not going to happen. Mind over matter.

Angela echoed her thoughts, whispering, "I have to use the bathroom," Lydia's eyes closed and she sighed. Her daughter squirmed and then squeezed her legs tight together. It was a feeling she knew all too well.

Jake met her gaze and then got to his feet, "We stick together. Mark and I will wait on the top step and you keep Angela company. It'll be fine." He looked over at Mark, "You can tell me about this *Minecraft* game while we wait. Let's have a normal conversation, try not to be victims."

She took a deep breath and led the way across the room, looking up the staircase before setting foot there. All was quiet up there...for now. Jake had secured the bedrooms, so they should be okay. Angela's fingers dug into her forearm and she turned to give her daughter a smile. It felt plastic and forced.

Her body grew tighter and more wary with every step higher. The creaking steps sliced through the raw ends of her nerves. The gaping door was just ahead, another two steps and still nothing had happened. She pushed the door wider and crept inside. Whatever had banged around in the upstairs earlier had left the bathroom alone, thank God.

When Angela followed her in she shut the door and stood with her back pressed against it. The only sound was Mark's voice talking to Jake. She closed her eyes and willed her heart to slow as she waited for Angela to finish. The toilet flushed and then Angela was beside her turning the sink tap on.

So far, so good. She took her turn, the sigh of relief not only due to her pressing bladder emptying but also that nothing scary had happened.

The sound of water started gushing from the tap over the bathtub made her turn her head to look. Lydia gasped. Angela didn't turn that water on, she was at the sink. She looked back at her daughter. Oh no! She was staring into the mirror above the sink, and her mouth had fallen open, her eyes also wide.

Oh God. It was happening again!

Jake's voice broke through, "Are you guys all right in there?"

"No! I mean yes..." She quickly finished and then lunged across the room to shut the tap off. Her heart was racing again, and she glared at the chrome tap handle. "Stop this shit! We've had enough!" She spun around and grasped Angela's shoulders. Seeing the mirror, Lydia gasped.

Oh my God! The reflection in the mirror! A dark-haired girl with deep-set eyes stared back! This was the girl Angela had seen! The ghost!

She pushed Angela to the side and grabbed the door handle. They had to get out of there! But the door wouldn't budge! "Open, damn you!" Her fingers twisted and she tugged for all she was worth.

"Mom!" Angela pressed into her, her fingers clawing at her shoulders.

She turned her head and screamed! The girl was right behind Angela! Blood streamed from the wound in her neck. Her hand rose and she came closer! Lydia pulled Angela into her arms and turned away so that she sheltered her daughter from the specter approaching. Oh God.

The thundering on the door was followed by Jake's voice, "Get back! I'm breaking the door down!"

Angela clung to her, her face hidden in the curve of Lydia's neck. Lydia twisted and she could see the girl's finger cross her bloody lips. She wanted them to be quiet? As if! "Leave us alone!" Lydia's voice sounded like a broken screech even to herself. Any more of this and she'd check herself into a looney bin.

Another two resounding thuds and the door burst open! Jake stared at her and then past her. His eyes bulged at what he saw. He grabbed her arm, and pulled both of them through the doorway.

She raced down the stairs right behind her daughter and son. So much for trying to be calm. The bathroom door slammed shut, and Jake's breath was hot on her neck, following closely.

When they entered the living room they scurried to the sofa gulping mouthfuls of air. Lydia sat between the kids, each arm pulling them into her. The picture of the girl was tattooed to her retinas! She'd never be able to rid herself of that face, the blood from her neck oozing fresh.

Angela's head lifted and she stared at her. "You saw her,

didn't you? She was there, in the room with us!"

She nodded. "The same girl in the photo. She was in the mirror and then she was there, behind you." She looked over at Jake. It was clear from the look in his eyes that he'd seen her too. "That's why you came running down earlier, isn't it? She was in Angela's room."

"Yeah." He sat back and then his hands threaded through his hair, becoming fists tugging handfuls. He was quite literally tearing his hair out. Now she knew how a person could be so shook up that they'd do that. His hands dropped and he looked over at her. "She threw a book at me."

"What?" Her head bobbed, gaping at him.

Before she could say anything more, Mark spoke, "What kind of book?"

She glanced at her son. Trust him to ask for specifics. Turning back to Jake, "Did it hit you? Where is it?"

Jake got up and threw a log into the fire. He turned to them and his face was drawn, worn out. "It's her diary from the looks of it. I was going to read it after we got out of here."

Lydia stood up, "Where is it? I think we should read it now!" She looked down at Angela and Mark, "I think she's trying to warn us about something. She signaled to be quiet when we were in the bathroom."

Angela's mouth dropped, and she shook her head. "Are you serious? This isn't bad enough, stuck in a haunted house? Now we need to read some dead girl's diary? This is totally crazy!" She folded her arms with a huff. "Reading a girl's diary is begging for trouble you know."

Mark elbowed his sister, "Like we're not in trouble now? How much worse can it get? It might actually help. Don't forget, I was the one who saw the mean old man. He's scary."

"I agree with Angela. Leave it alone." Jake took a seat again.

Lydia could feel her jaw tighten. Just because Jake thought it was a bad idea didn't make it so. "It's two against two, a tie. Got a coin? Let's call it."

Jake rolled his eyes but he reached in his pocket and pulled out a quarter, holding it up. "Heads we leave it, tails we read it, although I really don't see how that's going to help us right now."

She crossed her arms over her chest, and her chin rose. "Just flip it, already."

He shook his head and then tossed the coin high. The light of the fireplace glinted in a flash off it before it landed in his palm. He closed his fist and then planted his hand on his other one. He lifted his hand and sighed, "You win."

"Where is it?"

Lumbering to his feet, he mumbled, "I'll get it." He walked across the room, and when he came back he handed the diary to her. "Knock yourself out."

A faint whiff of lilac wafted from the cushioned cover and watermarks stained the pattern lilies. The raised, gold-embossed lettering had cracked in a few places. For a moment she hesitated looking at it. It felt wrong to be reading another person's private journal.

Mark tugged at her shirt, "C'mon, Mom. Read it."

She looked into his brown eyes and saw Liam in the earnest expression there. Her husband was gone just like this young girl. Both murdered. The amount of violent death she'd been exposed to in just the last three days was overwhelming. She feathered her fingers though Mark's hair. Any of them could be next.

Not on her watch. Taking a breath she shook the forboding feeling away. The girl had pitched it at the FBI agent. She must have wanted the journal to be read.

She sat down and opened the book. The first page was smudged and faded but she was able to make out the loopy script.

Property of Nancy Hawkins - PRIVATE (that means you!)

Angela nudged her. "See? We shouldn't be reading this."

Lydia rolled her eyes. She wouldn't mention the fact that Angela was hunched close to her, her eyes riveted on the book.

She turned the page and read out loud.

TWENTY EIGHT

Angela

Angela shivered and clambered closer to her mother as she began reading.

April 5, 1930

Dear Diary,

Happy birthday, ME! Sweet Sixteen. Thanks to Mom, I can now write my thoughts and feelings down. She slipped you, Diary, to me when we were making breakfast and told me to hide you. Daddy doesn't like secrets and you are absolutely my secret. I could hardly wait to get through the day to be able to start.

But where to start? This is my first official diary so I don't want to mess this up.

My name is Nancy Hawkins and today is my sixteenth birthday! Drat. I already told you that. See? I knew I'd mess it up. You'll have to be patient with me.

My mom is Daisy. She's really sweet to me, just like the

maple candy she makes! She wanted to name me Lily, a flower just like her name but Daddy wanted to name me after his favorite aunt. Nancy's a plain name but I'm stuck with it. I guess that's why she picked a book with a picture of a lily on the cover.

I have a younger brother, Jeremiah. He's twelve and spoiled rotten. He gets to do whatever he wants and never gets in trouble when he shirks his chores, which is often.

My Daddy is a preacher at the First Baptist Church down the road. He's strict. When he's not writing sermons he tends to the farm. We have cows, two horses and some noisy chickens. Jeremiah is supposed to clean the stalls, but of course he goes swimming, or hanging out with Billy Mullins. Anything but the chores. I've offered to help, but Daddy says the barn is no place for a girl.

Angela was already tired of the girl's story and her mother's droning voice. She snatched the book from her mother's hands. "This isn't helping. We need to find out what happened to her, not all these boring details." She thumbed through the book. There had to be over a hundred pages!

Mark grabbed at it but she held the book high, out of his reach. He whined, looking over at Mom. "She didn't even want to read it! Let me have it or *you* take it!"

But it was Jake who snatched the book from her hand. "I'll scan through it. She threw it at me, after all. There might be something toward the end that will give us a clue what happened. Why the old man went berserk and killed them all."

"WHAT?" Mom almost flew up from the sofa, her hands on her hips glaring at him.

Jake opened and closed his mouth a couple times.

"What the hell did you just say? You KNEW about this place? And brought us here?!"

"No..." He looked around the room, anywhere but at Lydia. "I..." He took a deep breath. "When the appliances were being delivered, some old geezer told me that this place had a history, that's all."

"Oh *really.*" Mom crossed her arms. "Just what kind of history?"

"He said something about some murders..." Jake sighed. "And that the place was thought to be haunted."

"What! And you just..."

Angela could only stare as Mom proceeded to give the FBI guy shit. He'd known the story and yet he'd still put them in a house that was cursed. She felt Mark sidle closer to her. His eyes were wide, and his jaw had fallen open.

He inched closer and whispered in her ear. Actually more like a low voice to be heard over Mom's screaming lecture at Jake. "I knew that old guy was bad. He killed his whole family."

Angela sunk lower on the sofa. She'd heard snippets of news broadcasts where a mother or father went crazy and killed the family, committing suicide afterwards. And here she was, sitting in a house where it had actually happened. A house where they were supposed to *live*! And they'd *known* it when they put them there!

The FBI were supposed to keep them safe. How in God's name was putting them up in a haunted house safe? What brain surgeon came up with that brilliant plan? She took a deep breath, clenching her jaw so tight her teeth ached. At this point she'd take her chances with the drug cartel.

She looked at her mother screaming at Jake. Her face was red as a tomato, and that vein in her forehead had popped out. A spittle flew from her lips when her mouth kept going. She'd only seen her mom this mad once, when another real estate agent had scooped her on a million dollar deal.

Mark stood up and pulled at his mother's arm. Tough to do since she was swinging them like she was using sign language. "Mom! Let him read it! Getting mad isn't going to help us. But that book might."

Mom's mouth snapped shut and her eyes flashed. But she sat down, her arms folded tight over her chest. "Fine!" She sneered at Jake. "Okay Mister FBI, read it! Then tell us how we're going to get through this alive!"

Jake's chin dropped and he looked over from under a creased brow. "I'm sorry. Give me a minute to see if there's any clue to...to deal with this."

TWENTY NINE

Jake

Jake's hand trembled with anger and terror as he thumbed the pages of the diary. He was pissed off to no end at Lydia for screaming at him like all this was his fault. For the love of God—who the hell would have believed that crazy story the delivery guy told him? He was scared shitless because…well, because that crazy story was true.

Not only were ghosts real—seeing that girl Nancy's spirit was absolute proof—but they were trapped in this house with them!

He flipped a few pages, skimming the handwritten paragraphs...

May 14th 1930

I can't wait to get out of this house. The day was going well up until we got home from church. Mom was going to make dumplings for the chicken stew but she'd run out of eggs. I went out to the barn to see if any of the hens had laid, but Daddy caught me coming out of the barn. I

thought he'd still be at the church and he'd never know. Oh was he furious!

After he finished beating me (he used a willow switch! Owww!) he sent me back to the house. I looked at him as he stood in the pathway, staring at the barn. He looked scared. I don't know why he was scared, I'm the one who got the whupping! What's in there Daddy doesn't want me to know about?

Jake's eyes narrowed. If it weren't for the grisly murder, this would just be the complaining of a teenage girl. But knowing how it ended, it might be significant. He flipped ahead a few more pages,

May 29th 1930

I was coming back from the outhouse tonight when I heard the barn door slam shut. I saw Daddy was coming up the path. He was walking funny and his face was red as a tomato. I don't know why, but it scared me. He'd been fine earlier in the day, so I knew he wasn't sick. I ran to get Mom to see what was wrong. She took one look at him and then made me go upstairs for the night.

So here I am Diary writing to you. Something ain't right though. I can hear Daddy yelling at Mom from the air vent in my room. And his words are slurred. He sounds like Willy Brown did when he got stung on the lip by a wasp. Mom isn't saying anything. Why would he be so angry with her?

Jake's gaze fell to the side. Kids on farms sure were innocent back then. Obviously her father was drunk. And he was a mean drunk at that. But the time period. In 1930, Prohibition was in full swing. Besides which, he was a preacher. But he wouldn't be the first hypocritical clergyman he'd ever seen. Was he brewing moonshine?

Lydia grabbed the wine bottle and poured two glasses. She handed one to him. "Don't just keep it to yourself! At least I read out loud."

He glanced at the kids before he spoke, "It looks like the father, this Charles guy liked his liquor even though he was a pastor. Things were strained between the daughter and her old man. A lot of this is her griping about him." He took a long swallow of the wine and set the glass on the floor next to him.

He went back to the book, skimming through it to find more references to the father. There was a lot of horseshit about some boy at school who she had a crush on. It looked innocent enough. Then he spied another entry that was different, the writing more cramped. He glanced over at Lydia and read aloud.

July 4 1930

Dear Diary, I'm so ashamed. I won't be able to look anyone in the eye ever again after what Daddy did. He made a total spectacle of me. Jimmy and I weren't doing anything wrong. We'd wandered off from where everyone was having fun next to the river. The band was playing, kids were running around screeching and you couldn't hear yourself think. Jimmy and I were within sight, just sitting on some rocks, watching some boats going by and just talking about how the summer was going.

Daddy came tearing over and started cussing Jimmy out. Then he yelled at me to go on home. He was so loud that people stared at us. I had to keep my head down as I went by them, breaking out into an all-out run once I was out of sight.

I knew Daddy was going to lay a beating on me when he got home so I hid in the barn, in the hayloft. I heard footsteps and I thought I was a goner, but some men came in. I didn't recognize them but they looked like river rats. They were real rough types, swearing up a storm and wearing dirty, raggedy clothes. They carried some wooden crates in and left them in an empty stall. They covered them up with hay and then left.

Before I got the chance to go see what it was they'd left, that rat Jeremiah came tearing in the barn and spotted me. As soon as he did he started yelling for Daddy. I don't know what Daddy was madder at, me sneaking around with Jimmy or being in the barn!

But he didn't whup me. Thank my lucky stars for that! For a preacher he sure knows a lot of swear words, the air was blue with them. He sounded just like those river rats!

He stayed in the barn the rest of the day, even missing dinner. I didn't miss him though. I don't think Mom did either.

How can I ever face Jimmy again?

Jake's eyes scanned ahead and his voice stilled. It was more of the same, the girl's embarrassment, how much she liked Jimmy, blah, blah.

Angela leaned forward and prodded the fire with the poker. "That father sounds like an asshole."

Mark gave her a sharp elbow, "Don't say that too loud. He might hear you." He looked over at the window and then behind him. "What do you think they're doing? It's been quiet for too long."

Lydia leaned over and patted her son's knee. "Don't look a gift horse in the mouth. The book was meant to be read and that's what we're doing. With any luck when the girl's story is known, the creepy stuff will end."

Jake watched them, and then his gaze locked with Angela's. From the look in her eyes, she didn't believe it either.

There was no doubt in his mind what the "river rats" had been delivering. Alexandria Bay was close to the Canadian border, and back then there'd been a lot of smuggling of booze going on. The preacher was not only a closet drunk, he was part of the smuggling racket. What better cover than running a church and having a barn for storage? He could guess the next part, but still he flipped through the pages till he came to the last entry.

September 6 1930

Dear Diary, The first day back at school went really well. Rather than laugh at me, my chums felt sorry for the fiasco at the 4th of July picnic. And Jimmy wasn't sore about getting chewed out by Daddy. If anything, he likes me even more.

Things have gotten worse with Daddy if that's even possible. He keeps watching me when he thinks I am not paying attention. And after last night, I know now why he yells and slurs his words.

I was so hepped up about the first day back at school, I needed to get some salts to settle my stomach. When I went to the kitchen to get some, he was sitting at the table cupping a mug of something. He grabbed at me when I went by him and I could smell it. Liquor. He forced me to sit on his knee and he kept telling me to watch out for the boys at school, that they only wanted one thing off a pretty girl like me.

Thank goodness Mom came in from the privy! It made my skin crawl the way he looked at me and the stink of him, his hands pawing my thigh.

When I left I could hear him cussing and yelling at Mom. Even Jeremiah was scared and came into my room for a bit.

I can't wait to get out of this house and marry Jimmy at the end of the school year. I know he's going to ask me.

He could see it in his mind, how the old man had gone off the deep end, not even trying to hide his drunken state. Even the girl, Nancy, had sensed something seriously wrong that night. He shuddered. Anything incestuous and predatory was so repugnant. And for the sickness to end in such violence. The poor girl, her brother and mom. The old man could burn in hell; he deserved to.

Lydia cleared her throat, looking down at her lap, "That

was the last entry wasn't it?"

Jake nodded and put the book down on the floor. "Yeah…"

Angela's eyes were wide. "Because after that, her father killed her."

Jake nodded. "Yeah."

Mark's head swiveled around the room, looking up to the ceiling. "And..he's still here…"

"Yeah."

THIRTY

Lydia

Lydia finished her wine and set the glass on the floor. For the last hour, things had been quiet. Angela could barely keep her eyes open, and Mark was curled up at the end of the sofa sleeping.

She looked over at Jake. He looked like hell. Hopefully, she didn't look as ragged. "I'll take the first watch if you want to catch forty winks."

He took a deep breath and then got up to throw another log on the fire. "Yeah." He looked at the kids and sat down again, stretching his legs out in front, resting his back against the sofa. "If you're sure?"

She nodded. "If it gets too much and I start to nod off, I'll wake you." The kids were first and foremost. Just get through the next four hours and get the hell out of there.

She stared at the flames of the log burning. It was mesmerizing how the flames licked at the edges of the log, curling around the sides before fading out. Her head jerked backward with a start and she gave it a shake. Watching a fireplace was a sure way to nod off. She sat straighter and took a deep breath to perk up. Just four hours.

She turned her gaze from the fireplace and looked over the living room and began to examine the layout with her sales agent brain for a distraction. Wide, solid oak staircase to the upper floor, graceful hallway to the dining room and kitchen, with a cozy room off to the side, perfect for a den or library.

Her mouth twitched in a scowl. The den was empty now, but it was probably where the father composed his Sunday sermons. Most likely with a fifth of whisky stashed in the desk. What a horrible old man to kill his whole family. The only one of them that had seen that monster's ghost was Mark. The youngest, smallest, and most innocent of them was the one that horrible thing sought first.

Jake's soft snores across from her, the crackling fire, and the peaceful breathing of the kids were a somnolent lullaby. She had to get up and move around to keep alert. She eased up from the sofa and tiptoed over to the den. She had never really checked that room out when they first arrived, and this was just as good a time as any.

When she stepped into the narrow room, a sharp creak from the floorboard pierced the air. She turned her head to see if she'd woken the kids. No, still out cold. She moved over to the window and pulled the curtain back to check the weather outside. It was still snowing but the flakes were bigger, falling slowly instead of the blowing blizzard earlier when they'd tried to escape in the car. That was a good sign; the storm was easing off, right?

Just as she turned to head back to the living room she froze at the sharp, grating sound from the ceiling above her. She lifted her head. It had sounded like someone dragged a chair across the floor above. That was Mark's room up there. It happened again—and louder. She looked over at Jake. Should she wake him?

It hadn't been loud enough to disturb anyone, they were all fast asleep. Compared to the nightmare earlier that shook the house, it was nothing. She could handle it. Let Jake sleep; the more rested he was, the better. There was still four hours to kill. She chided herself. *Kill* was not a good word to use this night.

She shivered when the scraping resumed. Something was moving around in Mark's room. Sure, Jake said he locked the door, but so what? She crept to the bottom of the stairs and peeked up. She couldn't see anything from the bottom, so climbed up two steps. The door to Mark's room was still closed. She let out a long sigh, only then realizing she had been holding her breath. God! She probably had aged ten years with the worry of being in this house.

Crik-k-kik-ki-kik! She jumped at the sound; louder now, and coming from the kitchen! She stepped down the stairs and then into the hallway leading to the kitchen. If it sounded again, she was going to find out why, damn it! This was ridiculous. The kids would wake up soon if it didn't stop. They'd been through enough. Hell! She'd had enough, too.

She'd take a quick look into the kitchen—maybe that would be enough to keep the…she gulped...*the ghost* at bay or something. Her eyes darted to the sleeping figures as she crept across the living room. Probably not her best idea, but they were all so damn wrung out. Just a quick look. The lights were on, after all.

From the entrance to the kitchen, her gaze flitted across the room. She jerked when it happened again. This time it was higher pitched, almost a squeal, filling the room from all directions. The hair on the back of her neck stood up.

Something moved in the corner of her eye. She looked over, but there was nothing there. There *had* been something *or someone* there! It had been in the kitchen and then gone without a sound! Her heart was beating so fast and hard she thought it would burst from her chest. What was it? The old man? He'd scared the shit out of her son but ran away from an adult, just like any bully would.

She took a few deep breaths to stop the shaking in her hands. Her knees wobbled like jelly when she stepped into the kitchen. Her mouth suddenly felt as dry as dust. Water. A powerful thirst rolled over her and she stepped to the sink and flipped the faucet.

She jumped back, holding her hands over her mouth. Oh God! Blood! It flowed from the faucet in a steady stream.

Her eyes were riveted to the horrible sight as the blood flow suddenly cleared and water gushed out. She blinked a few times to clear her head. It had been there! She edged closer, peering at the basin. But there was only a swirl of water circling the drain.

Had she really seen blood?

Enough! Her fingers splayed in front of her, backing slowly from the sink and out of the room. She was going to sit on the sofa and pretend this hadn't happened. No scraping, no dark man running from the room, no blood coming out of the faucet. Nope. Not happening.

It took all her willpower to not run back to the living room, but she kept her steps deliberate and soft. She was starting to lose it. She hoped she was starting to lose it…otherwise…*that really happened!*

Turning to head back to the living room, she froze at the sound of another creak from the stairs before her. Don't look. Don't look. Ignoring her own pleas in her head, she looked at the stairs. Please let it be just a noise. Just a noise.

Oh God, it was the girl! She was on the steps just a few feet away, her mouth gaping open in a silent scream. She looked as solid as any person, with blood smearing her nightgown from the gash in her neck. Silently, her hand rose and pointed behind Lydia.

The hackles on the back of her neck tingled. The sound of heavy breathing behind her registered in her ears as her nose was filled with the sour smell of whisky. She spun around, but everything had a surreal quality like she was in a slow motion film.

The breath caught in her chest and her eyes bulged seeing the old man. His eyes sparked looking at her from under a heavy brow. His mouth was half open, and his black tongue rolled over his bottom lip like an eel. He lifted a hand over his head, the ax in it smeared with gore.

"JAKE!" Lydia spun on the balls of her feet and raced to the living room. The kids!

Jake flew off the couch wide awake. He grabbed her shoulders but she twisted out of his grasp. "He's there! That old man!" She leapt to the sofa as the kids sprung to sitting positions and spun around to face the threat. She flung her hands out in front of her to ward off the apparition.

That wasn't there.

Jake gaped at her. "What did you see?"

She lurched forward and her hand clung to his arm looking past him to the dining room. "He was there! He was right there coming out of the kitchen!" She turned and pointed at the stairs. "Nancy. She tried to warn me." She looked up into Jake's eyes. "I swear, I saw them both!"

She burst into tears, and Jake took her in his arms, rubbing her back. How much more of this could any of them take before they were ready for the men in white coats?

THIRTY ONE

Jake

Jake held the poor woman, trying to calm her down. She was on the verge of a breakdown. And who could blame her? They were trapped in there until the sun rose, and even then who knew if they'd be able to get help?

The ghosts, or entities, or whatever the hell term you used...they were getting bolder. He didn't doubt that Lydia had seen both the girl and the old man. He'd never get that image of the girl rising from the bed, her head half off from the gaping wound in her neck. It was etched in his brain.

He shivered and then pulled back from Lydia. "It's not long now. We're leaving at first light." He turned her around, his hand light on her back, guided her to the sofa.

"Mom?" Angela reached for her mother's hand, watching Lydia with tear-filled eyes. "Sit here with us." When Lydia sank down next to her, Angela's arm went over her shoulders.

Mark leaned forward, "You saw him, didn't you? Now, it's not just me." He looked at Jake, "I think we should leave. Take our chances walking out of here."

Jake just looked at him, then at his watch. Only two thirty. If it were closer to dawn he'd agree with the boy. "No. We wait until first light. We'll get through this, I promise you." They were all worn out as it was. He didn't think they'd make it through the storm in the dead of night. They desperately needed daylight, especially if the snow kept up.

He glanced at Lydia. She was silent, staring at the fireplace, while Angela rubbed her arm. The roles had reversed and they had that damned ghost to thank for it.

Jake flopped into the chair and winced when the gun tucked into his waist dug in. If it were a thug, that gun would have solved the problem. But how do you deal with this kind of shit? Prayers? It had been a long time since he'd set foot in a church. The last time had been his wedding and look how well that had turned out.

He looked over at the family on the sofa. Angela's eyes were closed, and her head rested on her mother's shoulders. Lydia was having a hard time staying awake herself. Unbelievable. They were falling back asleep. Her head jerked and her eyes popped wide. She whispered, "How're you doing?"

"I'll manage." After a few moments he looked at her again, "Get some shut-eye. I got this."

She nodded and then settled deeper into the cushions, closing her eyes.

Everything was deathly still. Only the crackle of the embers in the fire broke the quiet. He shifted in the chair and took a deep breath. It was like there was sand in his eyes every time he blinked. A couple times his head fell lower and then bobbed up again. Lydia and the kids were fast asleep, and he was struggling to stay awake himself. It was like none of this was even real.

***

What? What was that? His head jerked up. The room was pitch-black. He couldn't see anything. Shit! He'd dozed off! He jumped to his feet and groped forward to where the sofa was.

He reached out and felt only the cushions. "Lydia?" He kept moving along the cushions, "Angela, Mark?" But there was nothing there.

Where were they?

He straightened, staring into the pitch-dark across the room. His hand yanked his weapon from its holster. For whatever good it would do. Something was very wrong. The back of his neck prickled.

Who took them?

Listening hard, he inched forward. "Lydia?" His free hand brushed the side of the archway, and he stopped short. Grabbing Angela's phone from his pocket, he shone the beam over the stairs. There was nothing there.

THUMP! THUMP! His heart skipped a beat at the pounding on the front door. Oh shit, was it the old man?

Sidling up to the door, he peeked out the window beside it and let out a whoosh of breath. Lydia and the kids! He yanked the door open before she could pound on it again.

A blast of icy air hit his face followed by Angela clambering to get inside. She stepped by him, "Shit! The frigging door locked behind us!"

He glared at Lydia, "What the hell were you doing?"

Shoving her way in, she looked past him to the darkened hallway and snarled, "Great! Just great. The power's out again." She had Mark by the hand and yanked him through the doorway with her.

Mark managed to slide in a soft murmur, "I had to pee." Lydia once more snapped, "It was just a quick trip outside! We weren't going back upstairs to that creepy bathroom." Her chin rose leading the way. "Nice job, keeping an eye on things, Jake. You were sound asleep."

He replied with an edge in his voice. "You should have woken me up! We're supposed to stick together!" For the first time he was glad the light was low. They couldn't see how his face was flaming with embarrassment. He had never before in his life fallen asleep on duty.

Lydia wasn't giving up, "Hey! I tried to! I called your name a bunch of times, but—"

"Stop it, okay?" Angela's hand flew up between Jake and her mother. "You two bickering isn't gonna help us." She pulled Mark after her, stepping over to the living room entrance. "Shit! The fire went out *too*?"

Jake was still standing there holding the door open like some kind of butler as they filed past chattering and bitching to no end. He went to ease it closed against the wind when the door flew from his hand and crashed into the frame with a loud bang. He jumped back at the suddenness of it. It slammed so hard the window glass cracked. He stiffened, staring at the jagged line in the window. It shut on its own? What the hell?

His jaw clenched tight and his eyes darted around the dark room. Message received, but fuck you, you evil piece of shit! Reaching forward, he grabbed at the door to open it again; icy pain speared through his hand as soon as it touched the knob. "Shit!" he yelled, jerking it back. "Owww!" He'd left a layer of skin of the surface of the now frozen metal.

It was like dry ice! A knot of dread gripped his gut when he turned to the family.

More scared than angry now, Lydia yelped, "What's wrong?"

Before he could answer, a blood curdling scream pierced the air!

It came from upstairs! Jake pointed his light to the top of the staircase. He peered blinking, seeing something in the low beam. A man's lower leg and boot had shown briefly and vanished. Thudding footsteps shook the ceiling above.

"NO! Please, no!" Another high-pitched wail pealed from above.

It sliced through Jake's chest. Again, the girl's terrorized scream shrieked. More shuddering bangs followed...then, the agonizing scream again!

"We gotta get out of here!" Angela pushed by him, grabbing the door handle. "Oow!" She jerked back, rubbing her hand. "What the hell?"

From above, the horrifying sounds of a life and death

struggle continued. Screams punctuated with gurgling pleas, the sound of bare feet padding on the floor above followed by heavy boots in pursuit, the crunching noise of the ax rising and falling on its victim played over and over in a maelstrom of awful chaos. Lydia and the kids huddled together with tears shimmering in their eyes.

Jake gaped at the ceiling along with the others, just as shocked, his brain as frozen as the doorknob. His years of training and experience had never covered this brand of shit-storm. That poor girl. For the last eighty plus years, night after night, year after year, she relived her own slaughter at the hands of that miserable animal. He flinched as the noises from above replayed again, the sound of the thunk of the ax head into flesh, ending with the crunch as it obliterated bone. And the girl's dying screams fading. That girl's mother and brother had moved on, but Nancy was imprisoned by that beast's unquenchable malevolence.

One way or another he was going to put a stop to that.

But first things first. He had to look after the living before trying to help the already dead. "The back door! C'mon!" He grabbed Angela, shoving her into her mother. Gripping Mark's arm, he hustled him along. On the way, he tucked his gun back into its holster, securing the retaining strap. The weapon was absolutely useless for what they were dealing with.

They ran past the kitchen to the small mudroom beyond, crowding into it.

Whatever horror had happened in that house was playing out again. He made a decision, praying it was the right one. They'd have to take their chances with the storm outside. It had to be better odds than staying in the house—all hell was breaking loose!

Angela was the first to reach the back door. She screamed when she grabbed the handle. "I can't! My skin's sticking to it!"

Lydia grasped Angela's arm, tugging for all she was worth. Jake's fingers clawed at Angela's prying them off the frigid metal. When she was free, he shoved his hand in his jacket pocket, using the cloth to grip the handle. He twisted, the vein in his forehead throbbing with the effort. Nothing was happening! The handle was impossible to turn!

Without warning, the house went silent. Quiet descended like a shroud. No more screams. Yet, this seemed even worse. Jake could hear his heartbeat thudding in his ears.

When footsteps resumed their thudding from above, Lydia grabbed the kids to shield them. He could hear the steps getting louder! The old man had finished his slaughter upstairs and he was coming down for them.

Lydia's face twisted in a knot as she yelled at him, "He's coming! Kick the damned door down! We've got to get out of here!"

Jake craned his neck listening. Every thudding footstep upstairs sent an ice pick of fear through his chest. Slow and steady, it lumbered loudly along the upstairs hall. Oh shit! How do you fight a ghost?

He handed the phone to Lydia and his body twisted, kicking the oak slab with everything he had. The shock went through his bones. He felt a "pop" and red hot pain spiked in his ankle. Shit! He broke something in there. But the footsteps were on the stairs now! He kicked it again...and again, adrenaline drowning the jarring jolts of pain.

"He's coming!" Angela screeched before joining him, battering her foot against the door.

All the while, the footsteps kept coming, closer and closer.

"MOM!"

At Mark's scream, Jake's head turned. It was the old man! His hand curled around the handle of an ax, and his white shirt was stained with blood. But it was the demented look in his eyes, sneering in the beam of the phone's light that made Jake's blood freeze. The old man meant to kill them!

THIRTY TWO

Angela

Angela screamed. *That thing*! That old man was right there! His eyes flared red while a leer twisted his bloody lips. He just stood there holding the ax by his side; thick, wet drips fell from it, plopping to the floor. He had them cold and he knew it! They were doomed...just like his family had been that night.

They were trapped in the mudroom, crowded in like animals! She peed herself, and it barely registered.

The lights flickered a few times and then came on. She blinked at the unexpected brightness.

Her body tightened. Now she could see all of that thing down the hall, the greasy strings of gray hair, the dark baggy trousers riddled with blood splatters and the ax head. Oh God. It was slathered with blood, and a bloody mass of hair caught in it. She forced her eyes away, the gorge rising in her throat.

Jake pushed her and he shouted, breaking through the trance of horror. "Get in the kitchen!"

She darted the few steps to the entry, dragging Mark by the

hand. Even though it meant coming closer to that...*that thing*, at least there was another way out of that room. They could run into the dining room. Yeah right! They'd go in circles being chased by that thing!

Mom was right behind her, coming to a halt in the middle of the room. Where was Jake?

She could hardly believe it when he yelled, "You aren't *real,* old man! Go back to hell where you came from!"

A high-pitched laugh sent a shiver down her spine. That horrid old man was demented! Hell-bent on a killing spree!

She looked over at the entry where Jake stood facing the thing. Every cell of her body screamed at him *Hurry! Get away!* Her throat froze solid, her eyes bulging as she watched. Jake stood his ground. What the hell was he doing?

Jake snorted, "You pretended to be a man of God, *you pig.* All the while hiding booze, lusting for your own daughter! You're nothing but a weak, hypocrite!" Jake scoffed. "You weren't much of a man, and you sure aren't much of a ghost!" He held his thumbs up to his ears and waggled his fingers. "Boo back, asshole!"

The thing snarled, and his footstep thudded on the floor! Angela gasped. Why was Jake goading the thing? He was crazy! That thing was going to kill him!

"Jake!" Mom shrieked. She grabbed Mark, holding him close to her chest, openly sobbing.

Time morphed into thick honey. Everything played out in slow motion while her mind raced at warp speed. She had to do something or else Jake was going to die. Then they'd all be picked off, one by one.

A distraction! She shrieked, "Nancy!" But it wasn't Nancy's face that flooded her mind.

Daddy? She blinked a couple times. Of course! He was dead too. "What should I do, Daddy?" Her eyes squeezed shut, but there was nothing. No message, no clue as to what would save them.

A thud on her arm made her eyes flash open. The shaker of salt floated end over end toward the floor. A scene of a horror movie she'd watched with Mark sparked in her brain. SALT! The hero had used salt against the entity. She scooped the shaker into her fist. In a flash she had the top off. White crystals filled the palm of her other hand and she leapt to the entry way! Snaking her arm by Jake, she hurled a handful of grains at the scary old man. "Take that!"

Her eyes widened seeing the thing stop. It even shrank back. It didn't like that! She tossed another handful at it.

Bellowing rage, it lurched to the side, and disappeared into the dining room. Its footsteps raced across the room, followed by a loud crash.

When she turned her head the old man leapt from the dining room. His eyes were fixed on her mother and Mark. He reached out his hands, fingers scrabbling at Mark.

"No!" She had to get to Mark!

Jake shoved her aside. Mark clung to Mom but the thing had him by the collar of his jacket! Mom's fingers tore through the fabric trying to pull Mark back to her.

Jake grabbed its wrist and in a sweeping twist, broke its hold on the boy. He stood facing it. "In God's name, leave us alone! In Jesus' name get the hell away from us!"

The thing's eyes opened wider and it paused. It was the chance she needed! She took the last of the salt and heaved it. The look of shock on its face as it staggered backwards gave her a glimmer of hope.

She darted to the cabinet to find more ammunition but Jake was one step ahead of her. He turned holding the box before him. She ripped it from his hand and sprung over to the entryway. A line of salt. That's what the guy in the movie had done. She poured it out and then raced to the other doorway to seal it with a thick line of salt.

The old man roared and she spun around to see. It—*that thing*—stepped closer. She braced herself, every muscle in her body quivering like a taut rope. But it stopped at the thin white line of salt. "It's working!" She grabbed her mother's arm, twisting her to see it.

"How did you know?" Mom swiped a tear from her cheek,

and her grip on Mark loosened.

Mark answered, "That movie." He looked up at Angela with awe in his eyes. "How did you ever think of it?"

Jake's voice was low when he interrupted, "Oh my God. Look at that."

Angela turned to where he was facing. She gasped. There, framed by the wooden entry was the girl—Nancy. Her dark eyes stared at them while her hand rose to cup the wound on her neck. Her fingers showed the blood when she held her hand before her. A ripple, like a pebble tossed into a pond water started to shimmer in the girl's chest. Angela watched in wonder as the Nancy's entire figure began to shimmer in rippling waves. A quick flash of the purest white pulsed out from her and held for a brief moment before fading. And when it faded, Nancy was gone.

"He's gone, too!" Mark's voice broke through their silent trance.

Angela could hardly believe her eyes. There was only darkness in the other room. The old guy had vanished. "What just happened?" She slouched forward, and her jaw dropped.

Lydia released Mark and then strode over to stand next to the doorway. She shook her head, as if she couldn't believe it was the last of the old guy. "Is it over? That can't be all of it."

Angela peered into the dining room to see if he was hiding somewhere in there. She could hear her breath in the stillness that now filled the house. But there was nothing to be seen or heard.

Jake's voice was barely above a whisper, "Anything's possible in this house." He looked at his watch. "It's just about four. In another hour it'll start to be light outside. It'll be safer to leave then."

Lydia barked a sarcastic laugh, "Safer? Anything's gotta be safer than this!" She walked over to the window to peer outside. "The storm's let up. I can just about see to the river."

Angela was still trying to process it all, but her mind was overwhelmed with what had just happened. She slumped into a chair and watched Mark settle beside her.

Her brother's eyes met hers. His face was pale making the freckles across the bridge of his nose stand out in stark contrast. He was a wreck with the bloodshot eyes and dark cusps rimming under them. "You don't think it's ended, do you?" he said, his voice shaking.

She leaned closer, "It was Dad, Mark. I know he was here when it was really bad. He made me remember that movie and the salt." It was a certainty she felt with every fiber. Hell. The horrible old man and Nancy had been in the house, why not Dad? Knowing this, her chest grew lighter. Dad was gone...but not really.

Mark nodded. "I know. I felt him too."

THIRTY THREE

Lydia

Lydia staggered to the table and dropped into a chair next to the kids. She looked at each of them with a sense of wonder. Her kids had been strong throughout this ordeal. If they could handle this, they could get through anything. She and Liam had done a good job raising them.

Still, a kernel of worry niggled in her gut. Was this a lull before the storm? Were the house and its ghosts finally done? She wasn't convinced. She'd never believed in ghosts until that night. She always thought that people who really believed in that stuff were more than a little nuts. She couldn't help but chuckle. Now she was one of *those people.*

She looked over at Jake who stood propped against the counter, his chin lowered, gazing down. She'd said some pretty harsh things to him, but in the final analysis he'd tried to save them. She forced a smile, "I wouldn't have taken you for a religious guy. It sounded like a prayer, when you spoke to that thing." There was no way she'd refer to it, that thing, as a "man"; whatever it was, it wasn't human.

Jake snorted and looked over at her, "I'm not normally religious. But after all this, I might change my mind about that. Actually, I might make a few more changes in my life. Maybe even my job." He looked down again, "I'm sorry about all this. You guys went through enough without the shit that happened here."

What could she say? He was absolutely right. "Will you tell them...your bosses I mean, tell them what happened here?"

He shook his head. "They'd never believe me." Huffing a fast sigh, he continued, "I'm not sure I even care if they do or not."

Angela spoke, "So, if they don't believe you, and us...they'll make us stay here?" She shook her head and ground her teeth so hard they clicked. "No freakin' way. I'll run away, so help me."

Jake pushed away from the counter, and his arms folded over his chest as he gazed at them. "You don't have to worry about that. No one will live in this house, ever again. You have my word on that." He turned and walked over to the doorway. "I'd better check that things have settled down. I don't know about you but I'd like to walk out of this house, not have to jump through a window to escape."

Lydia rose to her feet and followed him as far as the line of salt. The house might seem fine now, but she wasn't taking any chances. The kids nestled in close to her, watching Jake walk to the front door.

THIRTY FOUR

Jake

Jake's words were way more confident than he actually felt. When he crossed the line of salt—which had unbelievably worked!—the muscles in his neck tightened. Every step, every creak in the old wood sent a shiver up his spine. Where was the thing? Where had the old monster gone?

He slowed at the spot next to the stairway and looked up. Only a slice of light from around the bathroom door peeked out from above. Everything was quiet. Too quiet. When he turned, movement in the living room shot a knife of fear through his gut. He stepped closer and froze.

The old guy was in there! He stood in front of the black hole of the fireplace, holding the ax in both hands. He stepped forward through the sofa and then stood silently challenging Jake with a sneer. The smell in the room wafting from the thing almost made Jake gag.

"Is everything okay? Lydia's voice was high and strained.

The thing in the living room turned its attention toward the kitchen.

Jake backpedaled from the beast, yelling, "Stay in the kitchen!" He bolted for the door and tried the handle. It worked! The knob turned and he flung the door wide.

When he turned at the sound of running feet behind him, his jaw dropped. Lydia was racing up the hall, the box of salt leading the way. She emptied it in a flash across the doorway and then stepped back, her eyes wide staring at the thing.

The old man shrank and faltered before screaming "You'll die, bitch!"

Jake held the door open wide and yelled, "C'mon! Mark! Angela! We're outta here!" The thing in the living room glared at them, yelling obscenities, black spittle flying from its lips.

Mark was the first out the door, followed by Angela and Lydia. Jake watched them cross the veranda and then flounder in snow up to their thighs. But they were out. He peered at the horizon where a shimmer of pink tried to lighten the sky. There was still some snow coming down but it was waning.

He stepped down the hall and stared at the old man. He scooped his lighter from his back pocket and then flicked it, holding the flame close to the opening. "See this? Kind of what hell is like for your kind. Where you ought to be, you evil, despicable thing."

His other hand rose to pick at the wallpaper until a piece lifted. He tugged until a long strip flapped and then held the flame to it.

His eyes were narrow and he spat the words, "You're finished, old man. No one will ever live here again."

The fire lapped at the paper and then flared higher, catching the dry wood in its jaws. Jake turned and went through the door.

The old house would go up like dry kindling. It was done.

THIRTY FIVE

Jake

A month later...

It was Jake's first day back from two weeks laying on a beach, baking in the sun. He walked through the door with coffee in hand and took a seat at his desk. While he waited for the computer to boot up he reached for the small stack of mail that had accumulated.

A colorful envelope, hand addressed, caught his eye. He opened it to find a greeting card. The picture showed a surfer riding a crest of a frothy wave, the sun glinting off a tanned body. He flipped it open. Inside was written a short letter.

Hey Jake,

I hope this gets to you. I didn't know your address and had to send it to your work, if you're still there that is. We're kind of settled in a new house—"a modest ranch" in Mom-speak. My new school is big, kind of like the one I had before. Mark has even managed to make a couple of

friends, equally nerdy I'm sure.

Mom...well, she's not thrilled with the job at the post office, but it keeps her busy. I still say you guys should hire her for your real estate division whatever that is. She would make sure that you'd find the right house for people, if you know what I mean.

It's still hard without Dad but we're getting by, one day at a time.

If you're ever out this way, stop by to say hi. (A poet, huh?)

Angela Robertson

He sat back and took a long sip of coffee. The last time he'd read a teenage girl's scrawled notes, it had ended in tragedy for her. He took a deep breath and nodded. He could only pray this girl's story turned out better.

He swiveled in the chair to open his email.

THE END

Author's Note

One evening I was watching some crime show on TV. In it, the Witness Protection Program run by the FBI was mentioned. I turned to my dear partner Jim and said, "Wouldn't it be wild if they placed a family in a haunted house?"

Jim stared at me.

I stared back; and this book was conceived. I truly hope you enjoyed it; it was a pleasure for me to write.

While this book does not take place in Kingston, Ontario, we live right across the St. Lawrence River from Alexandria Bay, N.Y.. I've visited the area many, many times. It's a beautiful spot on the Thousand Islands, and yes, there really is a castle situated out in the middle of the river.

In the book publishing business, honest reviews are more important than ever; and that's true for the big, famous writers as well as little ol' me. I deeply appreciate everyone who takes the time to let others know what they think of my work.

ABOUT MICHELLE DOREY

A multiple bestselling author, Michelle Dorey has written more than a dozen spine-chilling novels featuring ghosts, haunted houses and the supernatural.

A voracious reader of the masters like Stephen King and Dean Koontz, her debut novel was inspired by attending a Ghost Walk in the enigmatic city of Kingston, Ontario, Canada. Crawley House was inspired by a true tale of a family's nightmare, living in a Victorian era home.

"Expect the supernatural when the bedrock of a city is limestone. When this ancient rock is surrounded on three sides by water as my home town is... well, you have the perfect setting for eerie events--which of course is my cup of tea."

Wife and mother, Michelle is also a dog lover, human to Suki and Ruby. She loves them dearly, but for the last eight years on walks, they absolutely refuse to enter grounds of a beautiful historic cemetery near her home.

Michelle has written two complete series, The Hauntings Of Kingston and The Mystical Veil. She's currently at work on her latest, The Haunted Ones--set in upper New York State.

OTHER WORKS BY MICHELLE DOREY

THE HAUNTINGS OF KINGSTON SERIES

The city of Kingston is enigmatic; where the line between this world and the next becomes quite hazy. A ghostly series inspired by this historic and sometimes mysterious place. Each novel is a stand alone:

Crawley House
The Haunted Inn
The Ghosts Of Centre Street
The Haunting Of Larkspur Farm
The Ghosts Of Hanson House

THE MYSTICAL VEIL

Twenty four year old trust fund brat Keira Swanson finds out that her family has secrets. Secrets of the dead...

Legacy
Heritage
Forsaken
Ascendant

PARANORMAL SUSPENSE

The Haunted Ones

Ordinary people confront malevolent spirits in each of these eerie tales...

The Haunted Hideout
A Grave Conjuring
Haunted By The Succubus
The Haunted Gathering
The Haunted Reckoning
Graveyard Shift

SPECIAL BONUS:

The first two chapters of

A Grave Conjuring

Book 2 of The Haunted Ones!

ABOUT THIS BOOK

Two orphaned sisters. A spirit without a grave. Can two orphans solve a murder before death claims another victim?

Ashley and Maya wish they could take back the hurtful things they told their parents before the deadly car crash. Two years later, the young orphans try to make the most of their new life with their lonely aunt. But the remote lake house in upstate New York doesn't feel like home without their mother's touch. When the girls discover a Ouija board in the dusty attic, they think they've finally found a way to tell their deceased mother how they really feel.

With help from a séance-savvy friend and a couple of neighborhood troublemakers, the girls summon the spirits… and an unsolved murder mystery. When a restless ghost terrorizes the household, the sisters know they'll never be free of her menacing presence until they help her rest in peace. If the girls don't find her body soon, the portal they opened will cast them all into the world of the dead.

If you like eerie supernatural encounters, coming-of-age friendships, and edge-of-your-seat mysteries, then you'll love Michelle Dorey's haunting story.

A Grave Conjuring is the second standalone book in the hair-raising series 'The Haunted Ones'.

A Grave Conjuring

By
Michelle Dorey

(Previously published as The Ouija Conjuring)

The Haunted Ones Book 2

ONE

"SHE ACTUALLY PAID MONEY FOR THIS DUMP?" Ashley shook her head. Despite the fact that the heavy packing box made her arms ache, she couldn't help pausing a moment, taking in the cracked vinyl floor and the chipped paint on the cabinet doors. Her nose pinched, smelling the mustiness. The previous owner had been an old man, and he'd left that "old person" smell in the house. The heat in the stuffy kitchen wasn't helping either. "Yuck."

Maya nudged her shoulder, "Quiet. She's coming." She led the way across the room to the hallway and stopped, adjusting the bins in her arms before going up the stairs, "It's not that bad. At least with the lake, we'll have something to do this summer."

"How are you girls making out?" Aunt Claire came into the kitchen and dropped a box on the counter with a resounding bang. "That's the last of it for this trip." She smiled, wiping her hands on faded blue jeans. "Well? What do you think?"

Ashley forced a smile, "You weren't kidding when you said it was a fixer-upper. The setting is pretty nice though." Still, she couldn't help wondering if perhaps Aunt Claire had bitten off more than she could chew with *this* project. Sure, she had experience doing renovations but this one was beyond hope.

"That's why I bought it, doll! You won't recognize it once I'm done. Who knows? We may even stay here. I never thought I'd be able to afford a place on the lake. This might be my only chance." Taking a deep satisfied breath, Claire gazed out the window at the backyard sloping down to the water's edge.

Ashley turned, hiding her disappointment. Yeah, they were going to be stuck here for quite some time. She walked out of the room to join her sister at the top of the stairs. Each step higher tugged her gut lower. The house was in the middle of nowhere, a fifteen-minute walk to the nearest neighbor. If it were next year even, when she could get her driver's license, it might be bearable, but not now.

She trudged into the room at the far end of the hallway. It was only slightly bigger than Maya's room, but at least the view was better, overlooking the lake as opposed to the driveway. Setting the box on the bed, she couldn't help but notice the quietness in the air. When they'd lived downtown, there was always a car or people going past. Here, it was deathly still.

Footsteps sounded on the stairs, and a couple moments later, Aunt Claire stood in the doorway. "I'm heading back for another load at the old place. Do you want me to pick up pizza or hamburgers for lunch when I'm in town?"

Before she had a chance to answer, Maya popped out of her room. "Both! You're not thinking of cooking tonight, are you?" Her dark eyes shone while a wide grin flashed as she slipped by their aunt, stepping into Ashley's room.

"Good point." Aunt Claire laughed. "After this move, I'll be too tired to cook."

When Maya flashed a crooked smile, her milk chocolate eyes sparkled with mischief; it was a shot to Ashley's heart. Sometimes when Maya smiled and moved a certain way, it stunned her to see how much Maya resembled their mother. Of course she'd inherited the chestnut hair and lean athletic build, which was definitely all Mom. Ashley was their father's daughter, tall with his strawberry-blond hair, and the same shade as her aunt's.

Ashley sighed. Now wasn't the time to get melancholy, thinking of her parents. It was a little over two years that they'd been gone, thanks to that drunk driver. Still, moments of grief could sneak up and ambush you when you least expected it.

She shook it off, changing the subject, "Leah will be at the old house when you get back there, Aunt Claire. You're okay with giving her a ride out here?"

Her aunt nodded. "Of course. She can help you unpack and get your room organized. Carol's volunteered to give me a hand when she's done work."

Maya twirled a lock of hair around her finger, looking up at their aunt. "No Lucas? I thought he'd insist on helping you get settled."

The smile fell from Claire's lips. "He wanted to but I put him off. He'd be more in the way than anything. Carol will be a bigger help." She grinned. "Plus, it'll be fun having a girls' night! Something I haven't done in too long a time."

She glanced at her watch. "I'd better get going. You girls will be okay here on your own, won't you? Is there anything else you need me to pick up when I'm in town?"

Ashley shook her head slowly. This was it. This would probably be the way the summer would go—she and Maya alone while Aunt Claire was off selling houses. Alone and...

She hurried to the doorway and called to her aunt who was halfway down the stairs. "The internet. Can you call the company and ask them to put a rush on it?"

Claire looked up and shrugged. "I'll try, but it probably won't do any good. You might be stuck without TV or your laptops until Tuesday." Her eyebrows arched above a wide grin. "You may have to read or play board games. I remember playing Monopoly for hours when I was your age."

Maya raced forward and laughed, "You had to. Were computers even invented back then?"

Aunt Claire's eyes narrowed but the smile was still there,

"Smart-ass. Yes, computers were around in 2005. I'm not that much older than you two! My parents weren't as indulgent with me. They actually set boundaries, if you can believe that."

"No way!"

"Totally! See you later. Call me if you think of anything you need me to pick up." Her footsteps were followed by the sound of the kitchen door closing.

Maya twirled on her heel and grinned. "Let's check out the outside. Maybe we can go for a swim before she gets back. I don't know about you but I'm melting. It's got to be almost ninety degrees in here."

Ashley blew at a lock of hair that lay plastered to her damp forehead. "Let's air this place out. We should have asked her to pick up more fans. How are we ever going to sleep without air-conditioning?"

She went over to the window and tugged on the lip of the frame. But it wasn't budging. "Give me a hand, will ya?"

Maya stood next to her, muttering as they strained to get the window to rise. "Probably the old guy who lived here never opened this window." It creaked and then rose up a few inches, refusing to go any higher. Her eyes flashed wide when she looked at Ashley. "You don't suppose he died in this house, do you?"

Ashley snorted. "Why? So what if he did? He had to die *somewhere.*"

Maya was undeterred, her gaze darting around the room. "What if he's still here? I mean as a ghost or something, haunting the place?"

It wasn't a thought that Ashley wanted to dwell on. Plus, she was the oldest and therefore the responsible one. "That's just in horror movies. That kind of thing isn't real, Maya." But even so she couldn't resist. With fingers curled in front of her, Ashley pounced at her sister. "Boo!"

"Shut up!" Maya sniffed and held her head high walking out of the room. "I'm getting my bathing suit on and going for a swim. You can join me or stay here with the ghost. Your choice." She laughed and then sprinted down the hall.

Ashley chuckled as she pried the cardboard box open to unpack. Maya was making the best of a bad situation. Her little sister was so much like her mother that it made her chest hurt. Mom had always seen the glass as half full, while Dad had been more pragmatic. It was time to be more like Maya and go with the flow.

Knowing Aunt Claire, they'd be moving again after a year or so. Nothing was forever. She knew that from experience.

TWO

TEN MINUTES LATER they stepped down the few rickety steps at the back door. Stalks of overgrown grass scraped her bare legs when Ashley made her way down the backyard to the dock. Like everything else about the property it was old with a few planks missing while the ones still there looked like they might collapse at any minute.

Her arm rose to stop Maya from going any farther. "Wait. Let me test it. If it holds me, then you'll be okay walking on it." She stepped gingerly on the first plank and when it didn't break she bounced a few times making sure it was safe before creeping slowly forward. The water on each side was shallow but dropped off at the end of the dock, judging by the deeper blue there.

"Hurry up, Ashley!" Maya huffed an exaggerated sigh before muttering, "I'm sure it's fine."

The board that Ashley tried next, gave way with a sharp crack. "Shit!" Her foot shot forward to the next plank, narrowly escaping a nasty fall. "See!" She glared back at her sister. "Maybe you should wade in from the shore. This thing's not too secure."

"Seriously? You're such a wimp!" Maya threw her towel down and then raced over the dock, her feet flying by the broken spots. She leapt from the end, curling her legs into her body for a perfect cannonball splash.

The dock wobbling under her feet from Maya's sprint destroyed Ashley's last attempt to balance. She toppled to the side, arms windmilling, falling into three feet of water. Her hips bumped against the sandy bottom near the dock, before she shook her head, spewing water and curses from her mouth. "You little jerk! I could have been killed. And you know better than to jump in like that! What if there was a rock or stump there?"

Maya ignored her, swimming farther out doing a smooth crawl stroke. Ashley gritted her teeth, and lunged forward trying to catch up. The little fool would probably swim to the other side of the lake if she didn't stop her. It was a good half mile across and while both of them could easily swim it, their aunt would be back soon. They were supposed to be unpacking.

"Wait up!" She slipped under the surface, pulling hard and kicking fast to join her sister. When she surfaced, gasping for air, there was no sign of Maya.

If you enjoyed this free sample, you'll love the rest of A Grave Conjuring

Available exclusively on Amazon!

Printed in Poland
by Amazon Fulfillment
Poland Sp. z o.o., Wrocław

53719019R00101